HER RISK
TO TAKE
(NOVELLA)

HER RISK
TO TAKE
(NOVELLA)

Toni Anderson

ALSO BY TONI ANDERSON

"HER" ROMANTIC SUSPENSE SERIES
Her Sanctuary (Book #1)
Her Last Chance (Book #2)
Her Risk to Take (Novella ~ Book #3)

THE BARKLEY SOUND SERIES
Dangerous Waters (Book #1)
Dark Waters (Book #2)

STAND-ALONE TITLES
The Killing Game
Edge of Survival
Storm Warning
Sea of Suspicion

Dedicated to Readers.

AUTHOR'S NOTE

I updated this series in 2021, however, the overall story remains the same. It's incredibly difficult to revisit old work so I hope readers like this version as much, if not more, than the original.

Content Advisory: this book contains sex scenes, cursing, violence (domestic abuse/workplace shooting) commensurate with most Romantic Suspense novels. For more information:
www.toniandersonauthor.com/content-advisory

Sign up for Toni Anderson's newsletter to receive new release alerts, bonus scenes, and a free copy of The Killing Game:
www.toniandersonauthor.com/newsletter-signup

CHAPTER ONE

IT WAS NOVEMBER in the Treasure State, the sky so blue it made the russet of the dead grass glow like bronze, and the few remaining leaves on the trees shimmer pure gold. The scent of dark, fragrant earth rose up, filling the valley, mixing with the pungent smell of horses, saddle soap, and leather. Cal Landon cinched the girth another two notches as the quiet bay mare turned her head to give him a disgruntled look. Morven was smart and easygoing, but lately she was getting fat and lazy. When the heated indoor arena was built, the mare was going to be invaluable in helping kids and adults learn to ride, but in the meantime, Cal figured he better give her some exercise. He'd saddled a roan gelding for Ryan and was waiting for the other cowboy to head out after breakfast. Cal pulled a hoof-pick out of his back pocket and checked the horses' feet, clearing away clumps of dried dirt.

He and Ryan were checking fences down near the reservoir today. Cattle kept escaping onto the road, and he didn't want them causing any accidents. *There must be a break in the wire somewhere.* He and Ryan could have driven down, but the horses needed exercise, and they both liked doing things the old-fashioned way.

The Triple H Ranch was owned by the Sullivans—Nat and his wife Eliza, and Nat's sister and brother, twins Sarah and Ryan. Cal had been close friends with Nat since school and had worked at the ranch after he'd gotten out of prison. Most of the time he managed to forget about that dark period of his life, and the Sullivans made it easy. They never judged him, never held it against him. He'd probably have screwed up years ago without their unflinching support. Off the ranch, some people went out of their way to remind him he was nothing but a murderer.

A breeze snaked down off the Flathead Range, the hint of frost in its teeth.

Fall was a quiet time on the ranch. They had a couple hundred head of cattle that needed shelter from the cold and a constant supply of food and water, but it wasn't a particularly onerous time of year. He and Ryan could pretty much handle it themselves with the occasional help from Ezra, when the older man's arthritis wasn't playing up. Nat and Eliza were busy overseeing the construction of the arena and establishing the stud side of the business.

Things were looking up for the Sullivans.

Cal grabbed the saddlebags, which contained an axe, a spade, a couple of hammers, nails and some coils of fence wire. Enough to patch up any gaps they found until the scope of a proper repair job could be assessed. He pulled on his work gloves and swung his leg carefully over the back of his horse. She danced for a minute, adjusting to his weight, then settled and rubbed her nose against the wooden corral.

Sarah Sullivan came out of the house carrying her doctor's bag in one hand and a pink *Hello Kitty* lunch kit in the other. His mouth went dry, the way it did every time he caught sight of her. She waved and sent him a happy grin. He felt the return smile on his face even as his heart raced. Ryan came out behind her, carrying his daughter, Tabitha. The cowboy strapped his little girl in her car seat, gave her a loud smacking kiss that made her giggle, and then headed over to Cal at a jog.

Cal watched Sarah drive away.

"You should make a move there," Ryan said as he swung aboard his horse.

Cal narrowed his eyes. "That's your sister you're talking about."

Ryan snorted. "Yeah, but I'm not the one who wants to jump her bones."

Cal ignored him and urged Morven into a trot past the ranch house, but Ryan wasn't done. Something the twins had in common was the inability to hold back anything they might be thinking or feeling. Most of the time it meant Cal didn't have to say more than two words all day, which suited him fine. But when that focus was directed at him? Look out.

"No one lives forever, brother." The wind whispered through the nearby aspens, rattling branches and making a shiver crawl over Cal's skin, despite his flannel shirt and sheepskin jacket. "Don't assume she'll still be around tomorrow."

Jesus, that thought was depressing, but Ryan had lost his childhood sweetheart to cancer, so no one knew better that life was short, and sweet could be snatched away in a heartbeat.

But Sarah Sullivan was too good for the likes of him. She was a doctor. He was an ex-con.

"I don't know what you're talking about." He dug his heels into the horse's ribs. She shot forward and Cal would be lying if he said he didn't get satisfaction from beating Ryan to the reservoir. But the guy still wasn't done.

"I know how you feel about her, you know. I see it every time you look at her."

Cal winced, then shrugged. Hard to lie to a man he'd worked with daily for the last decade.

"She feels the same way."

"She tell you that?" Cal shot Ryan a look.

"I just know."

Cal snorted. "You're an idiot."

"Right back atcha, brother."

Cal rolled his eyes even as he ran his gaze along the wire. He pointed. "There's the problem." A tree had come down where the fence cut through a small wood.

"You bring the axe?" Ryan asked.

"Yup."

Ryan rolled his shoulders. "Looks like we're going to get a good workout today."

Cal grunted. As long as he didn't have to talk about his *feelings* for Sarah, that was fine.

The sound of the horses' huffing breaths in the cold morning air was accompanied by the creak of leather and the jangle of harnesses.

"Remember what you said to me after Becky died?" Ryan asked quietly.

4

Cal froze. That was the first time he'd heard Ryan utter his wife's name since she passed. "I remember," he said.

"Sometimes all you can do is keep breathing…"

Cal nodded and looked straight ahead.

"You were right, Cal. Those words got me though the first few days, the first week without her—hell, maybe even the first year." Cal glanced at Ryan who gave his head a sharp shake as if to clear it. "I don't remember that time, at all. Just the pain, and the fact you told me to just keep on breathing." Ryan swallowed repeatedly. Cal's fingers tightened around the reins. "I don't remember Tabitha as a baby—without Nat's photographs I wouldn't be able to picture her at all." Ryan had totally ignored his daughter, unfairly blaming her for his wife's death. "Becky would have had my hide for that. Fuck, imagine if she knew about the rest…"

Cal closed his eyes at the pain in his friend's voice. It had been the worst time imaginable, and they'd almost lost Ryan too. It had taken nearly two years of drowning in alcohol and women before Ryan had come through the other side. Cal could hear the knowledge, finally, that Ryan knew he had to move on without her, without the love of his life.

No one should have to go through that.

Ryan cleared his throat. "So those words of yours actually saved me when I needed saving."

Sometimes all you can do is keep breathing…

The cowboy looked out across the silver water of the reservoir, the mountains reflected in all their glory. "The thing is, eventually, you need more."

Cal knew where this was going. He shook his head. "Nuh uh. Not everyone."

Ryan grabbed Morven's bridle, brought their horses to a stop and forced Cal to meet his eye. "Everyone. Even you."

They were almost at the woods now. Cal slipped from the saddle and ducked under the mare's head, leading his horse forward before tying her to a tree branch. He wasn't about to argue with Ryan about life or happiness or expectations. Compared to where he'd been, this was paradise, and not a day went by that he didn't thank God for the Sullivans and the Triple H ranch. And, if his dreams sometimes included a certain petite, sassy strawberry blonde? That was his business. Didn't mean he intended to act on it.

He took off his jacket. "Pass me the axe," he ordered.

Ryan held it out with a grin. "As long as you don't go all *Brokeback Mountain* on me."

Cal gripped the wooden handle and braced his legs apart. "I was thinking more *The Shining*, asshole."

"The Shining Asshole?" Ryan guffawed.

Thwack.

Cal poured his energy into the foot-wide trunk of the downed birch and prayed he was man enough not to put his fist through Ryan's pretty face. *Thwack.* It was great his friend was finally moving on after his own tragedy. It didn't mean anything had changed for Cal and he didn't expect it to.

CHAPTER TWO

November 23rd

S ARAH SULLIVAN PUT her arms into the sleeves of her down jacket, eased her feet into sturdy winter boots, and slipped through the kitchen door. One of the ranch dogs, Blue, snuck out beside her and looked up at her with anticipation in his liquid brown eyes, as if wondering what adventure they were going on now.

She rubbed his silky ears. She was going on an adventure all right, but she had no idea how it was going to turn out. It was three o'clock in the morning and once again she couldn't sleep. She'd lain there tossing and turning, thinking about her options. The problem lay about a hundred yards away in the direction of the woods. Searching for her courage, she stood looking out at the property she'd grown up on. Sullivans had worked the Triple H since her great-great-grandfather settled this land in 1889, the same year the state of Montana was admitted into the Union.

And this year, they'd almost lost every fence post, every single blade of grass. She'd almost lost the home she'd grown up in, her daddy's prized horses, her mother's fine china.

It had been a terrible time for them all, but they'd

gotten through it. They'd persevered. They'd endured. Because that was what people who worked the land did. Their salvation had come in the form of Eliza, and Sarah couldn't be more grateful to another human being, not just for saving the ranch but, more importantly, for loving Nat.

Her dad always said if it came easy it wasn't worth spit. But it sure was nice to catch a break once in a while.

Sarah had always been the "good girl," the one who worked hard, made good grades, and respected her elders. She had gone away for medical school but had missed the ranch. She'd managed to find a residency close by and moved home as soon as she'd finished her studies. Her college tuition had cost a fortune, and she owed her parents everything, but more than that, she was a homebody. She loved this land, figured it was the most beautiful place on the planet. When first her father, then Becky, became ill, her medical training had helped steer them through the process and understand their options. Afterward, with Ryan pretty much losing his mind, and then their mother suffering a heart attack, Nat had needed her, and so had her baby niece. Sarah had never regretted her decision to stay, felt almost guilty to be so blessed. She was proud of herself, of her job, and of her values, but she was sick of being the good girl. After months—if not years—of being too scared to go after what she really wanted, she'd made up her mind. She was done waiting for life to happen to her. This was her decision to make. Her heart that risked being broken.

It had snowed earlier—a foreshadowing of what was to come. This year's spring had been so late they'd barely had time to smell the flowers before winter had flung itself at them again, but she was used to it.

The change in seasons made her all too aware she was getting older, something she no longer took for granted. She saw death on a regular basis at work—she was an ER doc at County Hospital. But the last few years had brought so much personal heartbreak she wondered how they'd all stood it—three years ago her father had passed, followed by her sister-in-law who'd been the same age as she was, and finally, this last spring, her mom… Emotion welled up inside her, but she thrust it down. Tears didn't help. She was done waiting for thickheaded, stubborn cowboys to make a move.

A shiver of excitement lit through her as she trudged across the thin layer of new snow. It crunched beneath her boots. There was just enough to shroud the earth in white and mark her trail in a very distinct path to the door of one of the cabins. She didn't care if anyone saw the trail. She wasn't concerned about being subtle or secretive.

They no longer rented out the cabins to vacationers. They didn't want strangers wandering the property until all that noise from New York City had calmed down. *It's not every day a mobster is shot dead on your property.* So the ranch hands had moved from the bunkhouse they'd shared into a cabin each. Ezra took what had been Eliza's cabin, and Cal moved in next door. Sarah marched determinedly to his door.

A wolf howled in the darkness, making the horses in the barn whinny. She had a shift starting at eight. She was tired, but determined. Cal was so respectful around her that if she waited for him to make a move they'd both be in rockers before he even held her hand. Instead, she was going to rock his world.

The dog wagged his tail as she climbed up the two steps and crossed the narrow porch. She opened the unlocked door and carefully slipped inside. She closed the door behind her as the dog settled himself in front of the wood stove that gave off a low heat. She quietly filled it with fresh wood. Some habits died hard in this part of the world.

She took off her boots, took a condom out of her pocket, and draped her jacket on the back of the couch. She wasn't going to be put off with excuses about him not being good enough for her. She was prepared for everything—even rejection if she'd mistaken reticence for indifference. Taking a deep breath, she headed for Cal's bedroom. It was dark inside. Pitch-black. She heard the quiet, regular breathing of someone in a deep sleep. The room held the seductive masculine scent of the cowboy she'd been in love with for years. She slipped the clingy wool dress over her head and let it fall to the floor. She wasn't wearing any underwear.

Moving tentatively, she found the brass bedpost—and wrapped her fingers over the cold newel. What would she do if he rejected her? She bit her lip.

Fear of rejection had kept her worshipping this man from afar for years. Too scared to act. Too timid to make the first move. Now she was naked in his bedroom, and it was a little late for second thoughts.

She'd first seen Caleb Landon with her big brother, Nat, when he'd been thirteen years old, and she'd been a wide-eyed preteen. He'd been the town bad boy, easy on the eyes, a glint of the devil in his smile. She'd loved him even then, although it had been pure hero worship that had made her squirm like a worm on a hook whenever her brothers had teased her about it. Cal had earned his bad-boy reputation a year later in a desperate act that had taken him from their lives for ten long years. When he'd come back he'd been different. It had taken a long time for him to smile again, years for him to grow into the man he was always supposed to be.

She loved the lines on his face, the sharp features, the ultracalm hazel eyes that noticed everything. She moved along the side of the bed, placed the condom on the side table. His breathing changed.

"Sarah?"

He'd woken up. At least he had gotten her name right.

"Uh huh," she murmured, hoping to avoid a conversation that would end with him saying he didn't think about her *that* way, he thought of her as his *sister*. She eased under the duvet, slipping her hands around his chest to hug him. She snuggled against him, her cold breasts pressed to his fiery hot skin, stretching her legs out along his much hairier ones as she eased her toes between them.

"I must be dreaming."

"Maybe we both are." She kissed his back, slowly, gently. Trailed her fingers over hard compact muscles that had tensed to steel. She moved higher and kissed his neck, nuzzling his short hair, grateful for the fact he didn't pull away.

Emboldened, she moved her hand lower and found him already hard.

If he didn't start thinking about her *this* way after tonight then they were doomed and she may as well brace herself for a broken heart. She started stroking him, tip to root, and shivered in anticipation. She'd spent a lot of time imagining this. He seemed to be holding his breath. She used her tongue on his back, tracing skin she'd seen but never tasted. Then, just when she thought he was going to push her away, he placed his hand over hers and increased the pressure of her grip. He groaned and thrust against her palm, and she could feel his whole body trembling.

"I'm definitely dreaming."

Sarah had never been sexually aggressive in her life, but she wasn't a virgin either. She'd had boyfriends in college, but no one had made her feel as alive as this guy did, or as uncertain. She'd seen other women looking at him whenever they went into town for supplies. He was hot, and he wasn't a monk. She wasn't prepared to watch him end up with someone else just because she hadn't had the nerve to make the first move. As first moves went, this was a doozy.

She kissed his back, scraped her teeth over the smooth tanned skin, loving the feel of his unyielding muscles against hers. She could feel his taut body straining, hear the quickness of his breath as she stroked him faster. She nibbled his shoulder. The guy wasn't helping at all, almost as if he was afraid to break the spell. She was fine with that, the idea of setting the pace, of controlling this first encounter was exhilarating. She reached behind her and grabbed the condom, ripped it open carefully, rolled it down his length, growing wet with anticipation as she eased him onto his back.

Springs groaned as she straddled him.

"Sarah, I—"

He was about to tell her he didn't want this, and she didn't want to hear it. She put her finger on his mouth, and he was immediately quiet. She rubbed against him until he was concentrating on her rather than talking or thinking. "I want you, Caleb Landon. Inside me. Please, say you want me too."

His hands gripped her thighs so hard there were going to be bruises. She eased just the tip of him inside her, and he growled as she rose back up—teasing, definitely. Taunting, possibly. Daring him to take what she was offering—to take a risk on *them*.

She moved her fingers lower, cupping him, massaging him until she felt him quivering beneath her thighs.

"Don't you want me, Cal?" she asked, circling him again with her other hand. The words were supposed to be a challenge, but came out more like a plea. His hands finally moved, grabbing her by the ass and bringing her closer. He sat up as he pulled her down onto him; her eyes closed as pleasure blasted her. She sank down, taking him deep, and cried out as her body exploded. She came that easily.

That's what happened when you went years fantasizing about a guy and finally got him where you wanted him.

He started kissing her then, not moving although she could feel him thick and hot, filling her. He ran his tongue over her collarbone, then lower, capturing her nipple in his mouth. She wasn't big, but he plumped her breast with one hand and laved the sensitive nub with his tongue. Switching sides, he drove her crazy with the need to move, even as he held her immobile against him.

She squirmed as pleasure whipped through her. He growled as she ground against him, clutching him with her inner muscles when he wouldn't give her the movement she craved. Finally, fingers digging into soft flesh, he thrust into her. She threw back her head at the wonder of it, holding on to his broad shoulders, wishing she could see him, knowing that if the lights were on Cal wouldn't be able to look her in the eye, much less screw her senseless.

She intended to change that.

He shifted beneath her, anchored her to him as he got onto his knees and followed her down so she was on her back and he was cradled between her thighs. He spread her knees wide and thrust deeper, harder.

Her nails dug into his shoulders with each movement.

She'd expected Cal to be a gentle, controlled lover—he did everything else with such slow reverence, especially around her. He treated her like she was sweet sixteen and never been kissed. But this was wild, this was ferocious, and she was right there with him, nails scraping his skin, striving to get even closer as he pounded into her body with no more reverence than a stag rutting in the forest.

She loved it. The pleasure was building again. The tingling anticipation and hunger for a climax spreading and making her wild and feverish as she clung, sweat making his body slick and hard to hold on to. She felt her orgasm build. Like a slow-rolling tsunami it swelled higher and then crashed over her just as Cal stiffened above her and poured himself into a yell that seemed to rip free from his soul. Her heart pounded, her pulse raced. She wrapped her legs around his waist even as he pulled out and lay on top of her.

Slowly the silence built. Thick and deafening.

Crap.

She didn't want to hear his regrets. She started kissing him again, slowly, tenderly, hoping he wasn't about to tell her this whole thing had been a massive mistake.

CAL HAD THOUGHT he was dreaming. He often dreamed about Sarah. Sexy, naked, X-rated dreams that would get his ass kicked and fired if Nat ever found out—not that he had any intention of sharing those dreams with either of Sarah's brothers. Dreams he had no business having, even in his subconscious. But he couldn't control them and had learned to live with them, knowing it was all he'd ever have so he may as well enjoy them.

So, until she'd straddled him in the darkness, and he'd touched the softness of her inner thighs, which had felt a million times more mind-blowing than he'd imagined possible, he'd believed he was having a really vivid, unbelievably fabulous fucking dream.

Then she'd spoken. *I want you, Caleb Landon. Inside me. Please, say you want me too.*

Want her?

Want her?

His heart raced as he lay on top of her. He must be crushing her, but he didn't dare move, terrified of what she'd say. He closed his eyes. He'd wanted her for years, but she was his best friend's little sister and an upstanding member of the community. He was nothing but an ex-con cowboy with blood on his hands. Enough people hated him and were more than willing to destroy anything in his life he cared about—if he gave them the chance. No way was he giving anyone the chance to hurt any of the Sullivans, especially not Sarah.

Her warmth curled around him as her chest rose and fell. Damp skin clung to his. Her hair brushed his cheek, the scent fresh and clean, like a pine forest in winter.

Shit.

Sarah was not some woman who'd come on to him in a bar. She wasn't some no-name one-nighter, which was all he usually allowed himself. She was one of his best friends. Christ, who was he kidding? She meant more to him than he wanted to acknowledge, even to himself.

What the hell had he done?

Taken her with all the finesse of a teenage virgin—although to be fair she had crawled into his bed and wrapped her fingers around *his* morning glory. God, even the memory had him growing hard again. He went to pull away, but her lips found the corner of his eye and the caress was so sweet, so loving he couldn't move. It held him in place as surely as iron bars ever had. Her tongue touched his ear, drawing out a shiver that was almost painful. Her hands ran down his back, fingers splayed over his hips and digging into his ass. He was planted between her legs, and the need to have her one more time crawled through his blood like an addiction, begging him to do it again.

He was so screwed.

He pulled back and dealt with the condom. Grabbed another from a box inside the drawer. They weren't even his. He assumed Ryan had used this place to bring back women before Cal had moved in this summer. The sell-by date was good though. He'd checked. Talk about optimistic.

"For a moment, I thought you were going to run away…" He heard a smile in her voice; he also heard the uncertainty. *She* should be running away. Fast and furious.

He wasn't sure what she was doing here, besides the obvious. There was no way he could give her anything except a little pleasure. But he couldn't tell her that. No way could he hurt her. The thought of putting disappointment in this woman's eyes made his gut ache. She was the single-smartest, hardest-working person he'd ever met. That included every cowboy, rancher, lumberjack, farmer, or goddamned cop on the planet. She never stopped. Either at the hospital, here at the ranch, or helping take care of her niece and the family. She never took a vacation. Never dated. Didn't have time to date. Damn. No wonder she was horny.

He could give her this. As long as no one knew, as long as she didn't become a target.

He wanted to turn on the lamp but didn't want her

looking at him, seeing his tattoos, a constant reminder of what he'd done and where he'd been. Of the kind of man he really was. He didn't want to watch desire fade to revulsion. He pulled the curtain open and let the moon light up the room with a faint silver glow. She lay on the bed, legs spread, hair in a messy cloud on the covers as she looked at him. Not even vaguely self-conscious or shy.

Not what he'd expected.

A smile curved her lips, and he had to shake his head to prove he really wasn't dreaming. Maybe someone had slipped something in his beer? Whatever it was, he'd happily buy a lifetime's supply.

They'd have to keep this a secret. They lived in the middle of nowhere, isolated and secluded. No one had to know. She didn't need to be tainted by association as long as they kept this between the two of them. He picked up her foot and kissed the inside of her ankle. She jolted. He'd forgotten she was ticklish. He trailed his mouth up her limbs. She was small, perfect. Slim, curved, beautiful, naked and, *fuck*, really here. His blood started racing again, but it was more incredible this time, because he knew it was real, it was actually happening. She'd come to him. He'd never expected her to, but she'd come to him, and he was torn between wanting to yell out his happiness to the world and sending her away so none of his tarnish rubbed off on her.

Her eyes were a cool blue-gray in the daylight, but right now they were dark as midnight as she watched him come closer and closer to a part of her body he wanted to taste.

She leaned up on her elbows to watch as he dipped his tongue along the sensitive skin at the seam of her leg. His skin was dark against the paleness of hers. The scent of her filled his nostrils and blew his mind. The taste of her flooded his mouth, and he knew he'd never get the essence out of his brain. It would drive him crazy forever, just knowing her flavor. The thought had him sinking his tongue deeper, loving her, teasing her, pressing against her clit until her jaw dropped, her head fell back, and she gasped. "Oh, God. Don't stop."

He didn't intend to.

Not yet.

He shifted her up the bed until her knees were draped over his shoulders, and he was eating her up with small bites and licks until she began trembling on the edge of release. He wanted to torment her for hours, but her hands crept between his legs, and she found him again, her fingers strong and agile—knowledgeable. His eyes crossed, and he almost came on the spot.

She was nothing like he'd imagined. She was infinitely more.

He lay her down and explored further, sweeping her belly button with his tongue before moving higher to feast on her breasts. He cupped and licked, watching her nipples tighten in the moonlight. Her hips undulated as her hands stroked him. He wished they could do this forever. Didn't want to think about why they couldn't.

She grabbed the condom from wherever he'd dropped it. Ripped it and rolled it over him with practiced fingers.

"You've done that before," he said.

She cocked a brow at what had to be jealousy darkening his tone. "Every time I've ever had sex, Cal. I do not want to be up on that pedestal. It's a cold and lonely place up there. I'm a flesh-and-blood woman like any other and want a flesh-and-blood man to keep me warm. Think you can handle that?"

It was cold down in the gutter too, and maybe for right now they could enjoy each other.

"The idea of another man touching you..." He closed his mouth. The thought of Sarah with anyone else made him crazy, but that admission gave away too much about how he truly felt. One day she was going to fall for and marry some other guy. He'd have to deal with it then, but he didn't have to deal with it now. Instead, he pushed against her, working his way inside, filling her until she gasped and clutched, those fingers digging urgently into his backside. She squirmed around him, and it felt amazing.

"Enough?" he asked.

"No. No!"

He drove forward until he was planted to the hilt, surrounded by wet molten heat that made him want to weep. They were face to face, his eyes lined up with her eyes. His lips lined up with her lips.

He dipped his head, and his heart shattered when she rose up to meet him, kissing him gently, reverently, like he was special. He kissed her back, keeping it light, exploring, committing her shape and taste to memory. She started moving her hips, urging him on, but he was stubborn and slowed it right down until she was as languid as melted wax, and then he finally started moving again. Slowly, surely, driving her up, increasing the pace, making her cry out, making her beg before he finally let her fly. And he was right there with her, soaring off the edge of the cliff into darkness, knowing he was going to crash and burn, but not willing to swap this moment for anything this side of heaven.

Nothing would ever be the same again.

And in that moment, he didn't care.

CHAPTER THREE

One month later...

SARAH WAS ENTRANCED by the patterns of ink that snaked from Cal's elbow down to his wrist. He'd had the tattoos professionally redone not long ago, no color, simple dark indigo against suntanned skin. She wasn't exactly sure what the tattoos were of, because he refused to let her see them up close. At some point during the night, she'd left the light on in the bathroom and now it filtered through, and she could make out scales, talons and possibly a fish on his left arm.

It was early. He was asleep—exhausted after hours of lovemaking. Sometimes it was as if they were trying to make up for all the years they'd missed. Other times it was as if they were cramming a lifetime of loving into a few short weeks.

She'd come to his bed every chance she'd gotten over the past month. There were moments when she thought he was going to turn her away, but he hadn't done so yet. He was getting a little less reserved around her, starting to trust her more, but he still wasn't willing to bring their relationship out into the open. Like most cowboys Cal was stubborn, and like most horses he could be led, but he sure as heck couldn't be pushed. Patience and persistence were what she needed, and she had both in spades. She leaned closer to trail her lips over the prominent bone at his wrist and worked her way up his arm.

"What are you doing?" he asked groggily.

"Enjoying your tattoos."

He tried to jerk his arm out of reach, but she stopped him.

"Please don't. I want to see."

His lips pinched together but after a long, tense moment he capitulated and held his arms stiffly at his side. As relaxed as one of the ranch dogs on the scent of a rabbit. She sat up and dragged his arm across her lap. "What's this?" The lighting still wasn't great, and it was hard to make out.

Cal's gaze wandered, and he seemed to be having a hard time concentrating on her question, probably because she was naked. She stroked one sinuous rope of blue scales that coiled around his flesh. She followed the trail with her fingers and raised his arm to see that it ended in an arrowhead tail.

He cleared his throat. "It's the dragon's tail."

"Dragon?" She was surprised. She hadn't imagined practical Cal Landon would have something as mythical as a dragon etched on his skin.

"What's wrong with a dragon?" he asked in a low growl.

She laughed and found the dragon's head. It was a fierce-looking creature. She kissed it and moved on to explore what looked like carp in a pool beneath the mountains. "Did you do the design yourself?"

"Me?" He gave a slight smile. "Stick figures are the limit of my artistic abilities." He cocked a brow. "This time I left it to the professionals." He tried to pull away, but she held tight, and he narrowed his eyes at her. She knew it was hard for him to let people in, but she wanted him to know he could trust her.

"They're beautiful, Cal."

"I had them done to replace the ones I got in prison." His tone was hard with self-recrimination in case she hadn't gotten the reference the first go-around.

She held his gaze. "I liked those ones too."

He blinked.

"What? Why wouldn't I like them?" She was naked in his bed, and he still had this holier-than-thou image of her. Crazy. "You know what else those tattoos are? They're *hot*."

His eyes widened as she trailed his arm over her thigh. She knew she was shocking him but figured he deserved it for treating her like she might faint at the least little reminder of his past. It wasn't like she hadn't known him before he'd gone to jail, and all these years afterward. She wasn't some death-row groupie. She was a practical, intelligent woman. She decided to shock him further. "I always wanted a tattoo, but can't decide exactly what I want...or where I wanted it. Maybe here?" She touched her outer thigh with his warm hand. "Or here?" She shifted until he was touching her somewhere much more intimate. She laughed as he grabbed her and rolled her beneath him. One way or another she was going to knock down this cowboy's walls and make him lose his reserve. Maybe then he'd finally understand that she loved every damned inch of him, tattoos, past, and all.

———————

CAL SLEPT IN so he skipped breakfast. He didn't want the horses to go hungry.

Being late was getting to be a habit, one he wasn't proud of. He'd add that sucker to the list. Sarah had been coming to the cabin most nights for the past month, so neither of them had been getting much sleep. He kept intending to tell her to stay away. Had braced himself that second night to be aloof and unwelcoming, until she'd taken off her coat and revealed she was stark naked underneath.

Resistance had proved to be futile.

He didn't want people finding out she was slumming. But the woman was like opium and once he'd tasted her he couldn't stop thinking about her. About them. Together.

He shook his head. There was no *them*. She was...*delusional*. It was the only word that came to mind.

He finished putting feed into Shadow's bucket. He'd already let her two foals out into the attached paddock to give them some exercise and the mare some peace from exuberant male children. She'd adopted little Red after his mother died during a foaling gone wrong last spring. The memory still made Cal alternate between pissed and heartbroken. The mare had died needlessly, and Nat had been forced to deliver the foal by improvised caesarian.

25

He ran his hand down Shadow's cheek, and she rubbed her head against his shoulder. She'd be weaning the foals soon. Her son, Silk, wasn't a pure-bred Arabian like Red, but he was gorgeous American Morgan and seemed to have a calming influence on the high-strung aristocrat with his pure Egyptian bloodlines and nose for trouble. They'd probably keep both colts, although Cal figured Silk would be lucky to keep his crown jewels. Only so many stallions the ranch could handle—even though they were starting to make a success of the stud business.

They'd made plans to build a small lab, and Nat was investigating specialized equipment for freezing and storing sperm, maybe even developing a cryogenic storage facility for other peoples' stallions and prize bulls. Considering the Sullivans had almost lost this place back in the spring, it was a damned miracle they were still up and running—a miracle that had come about thanks to Eliza.

He heard a noise outside and knew the contractors building the new indoor arena had shown up. He usually tried to be done and out on the land by the time they rolled up in the morning—not hard considering they generally didn't arrive until after ten. But Eliza had been on their case to get the concrete foundations poured before it became too damned cold. Frankly, not many men argued with Eliza—except maybe Nat. He was a brave man.

He heard voices as someone came into the stables— Eliza, then a low rumble as Nat teased her about something. Laughter turned into a squeak as Nat presumably pulled her in for a kiss and then as the silence lengthened, Cal clanged the bucket quietly against the wall, not wanting to interrupt anything too intimate between a man and his wife.

The thought made his chest feel hollow.

He stepped out of the stall and forced a smile at two of the most important people in his life.

"Hey, you skipped breakfast again. You trying to lose weight?" Eliza teased him. She had on worn-out jeans and a thick wool sweater, a stretchy hat pulled low over her dark hair. For some reason she was always trying to fatten him up.

Nat just shook his head. Eliza walked toward Cal, her limp not as pronounced in the morning as it was at night when she was tired. Her thighbone had been shattered by a bullet. It had taken a long time to heal—actually she was lucky to be alive, period. She had more screws and plates inside her leg than the bionic woman. Not that she let it slow her down—which was pretty much the only thing she and Nat argued about.

She pushed herself too hard. Never knew when to quit. Sarah was the same—worked herself to the bone and then wasted precious sleep time messing around with him. Sarah wanted to tell everyone about their relationship, but he wouldn't let her. He'd have to end it soon, before she got the wrong idea about them having a future together. It would sting, but she'd get over it. He clenched his fists around the handle of the bucket. "Slept in."

"You seem to be doing that a lot lately." Eliza grinned. "Anything we should know about?"

She was teasing, but Cal looked away, uncomfortable. Nat was his best friend, but if the guy found out the things he did to his sister when the sun went down he'd be pissed. Any man would.

"Leave him alone." Nat wrapped his arms around his wife's waist. "Ever since you got hitched you want everyone else hooked up and happy."

She turned and kissed her husband's cheek. "Nothing wrong with hooked up and happy. Should we tell him?"

Cal's brow jerked. He wouldn't ask even though Eliza loved to drag out the suspense. He believed in privacy. Didn't mean he wasn't full of curiosity, but he wouldn't beg and he didn't gossip.

Nat grinned. "He's going to find out soon enough anyway—not to mention I need his help to keep you out of the saddle for the next nine months."

"You're pregnant?" Cal grinned. He knew they'd been trying for a baby. The whole world knew they'd been trying for a baby, which was the reason he'd wanted to make some noise before they got naked in the stables.

Eliza's whole face glowed with happiness. She nodded, then frowned at Nat. "Why do I have to stay out of the saddle?" Eliza didn't often pout, but this expression came close.

"Because you don't stay *in* the saddle," Nat said between gritted teeth.

This was true. Cal didn't know anyone who fell off a horse as regularly as Eliza seemed to manage.

"What if I want to ride?" she said belligerently.

"Be my guest," Nat said with a wicked grin.

She blushed as Cal choked on a cough.

"How about we compromise?" Nat sobered. He seemed to have learned patience and diplomacy over the last few months. Probably because his wife carried a gun. "How about I take you out on Winter every once in a while?" Winter was a rare, gray, oversize American Morgan stallion who was even-tempered and steady.

"Fine." Eliza leaned up and kissed Nat's cheek. Then squeezed out of his arms and hugged Cal. He wrapped his arms around her, happy for them, but inside his own sadness was growing, and with it a sense of envy he'd never experienced before. He wanted to be part of all this, he wanted to accept the position they offered him in the family, but he couldn't. It would be too selfish, and if anything happened he wouldn't be able to live with himself.

A desperate night nearly twenty years ago had marked him. He'd killed a man, and that man's family wanted revenge. There were people who would hurt him any way they could. Including targeting the people he loved. They'd cornered him a couple of times over the years, attacked him, slashed his tires, even stole his old beater of a truck. It had been found burned out and abandoned. Nowadays, Cal stuck closer to the ranch, which was secluded and remote, but it was only a matter of time before there was another confrontation.

"I'm really happy for you." He squeezed her gently and closed his eyes, wishing he'd made different choices, anything other than swinging out and hitting the bastard who'd been beating his mother.

He let Eliza go and left them to it. He went off to the barn to feed the other horses, noting the speculative glances of the contractors who milled about next to a giant cement mixer. As far as they were concerned he was another hired hand on this ranch—which was exactly what he wanted them to think. He recognized one of the guys there as a good friend of his stepbrother. He bet he'd be feeding Terry any information worth telling.

Cal would never let anything bad happen to the Sullivans, especially not to Sarah. He'd protect her, even if it meant cutting out his own heart.

———

THE BALLS OF Sarah's feet throbbed after the double shift from hell as she parked on Main Street. One of the attending physicians at County had broken her ankle and been unable to come in to work. Worse, the good doctor was also going to be off tomorrow—Christmas Eve—which meant, rather than spending the day decorating the house and preparing the turkey, Sarah was going to be stuck back at work. Eliza had offered to cook Christmas dinner, but frankly, as much as Sarah loved her sister-in-law, her cooking skills sucked. Plus, Sarah *wanted* to do it. She'd stay up all night prepping veggies if she had to. She thought of her mother, and the importance of carrying on traditions, traditions that she was determined to pass on to another generation of Sullivans, from Tabitha to this new baby Eliza was expecting.

Warmth spread over her. She was excited to be an aunt again, especially after the ordeal Eliza and Nat had been through on their road to happiness. If anyone deserved some good news it was the two of them. But she'd be lying if she said it didn't intensify the pang of wanting her own child, her own family, even if the man she wanted it with was proving ridiculously stubborn about their relationship.

Maybe she should make an announcement in the local paper. Sarah Sullivan loves Caleb Landon and doesn't care what anyone else thinks.

She grimaced. He'd hate it.

She didn't know exactly why he was so guarded, but right now she was taking it one furtive step at a time.

She hurried along the sidewalk, heading for the best jeweler in town—the only jeweler in town, actually, but they had amazing inventory.

She blew out a sigh and stopped in front of the store window. A selection of rings sparkled beneath the fairy lights, the effect making her breath catch in delight. Her eye snagged on a gorgeous circular design in white gold with an intricate weave of tiny diamonds inside. She sighed so hard her breath fogged up the glass. No way Cal could afford one of those even if he wanted to, and no way she'd expect him to waste his money on something so…*incredibly gorgeous*. Maybe she should just buy her own damned ring and be done with it.

She pushed inside and was hit by a wall of warmth and the thick scent of something sweet, like blackberries and cloves. Whatever it was smelled delicious and reminded her she was hungry.

Mr. Rozen smiled and waved her over to where he stood behind the wide glass counter. His wife was serving another customer.

He pulled out an array of boxes from underneath the counter. "They just came in," he told her, reverently opening each one.

She reached out and laid a finger on the intricate detail of a cowboy atop a horse. "Oh, they're perfect." A month ago, she'd ordered four silver belt buckles, one for each of the men on the ranch—Cal, Nat, Ryan, and Ezra. The latter should have retired years ago but had stuck beside them even when they couldn't pay him. Since Eliza had arrived Sarah had been able to start spending her salary on what she wanted, rather than pouring every penny into their debts. Sarah was saving up for something special of her own now. It was a surprise for everyone, and would keep her closer to home and hopefully decrease her workload.

She might actually get to have a life.

The buckle she'd chosen for Nat had a wolf on it, howling at the moon. For Ezra she'd chosen a very traditional bucking bronco, which she hoped he never got on because she didn't want to fix more broken bones. Ryan's had two horses, side by side. He'd think it was because they were twins, but she was hoping he'd find his own happy ending—a second chance really—after everything he'd lost. For Cal she'd been drawn to that lone cowboy sitting atop a horse in front of a sunset. A lump of emotion grew in her throat. Even in a crowd he always seemed so isolated. She ached for him. Ached for herself because she wanted to see him smile more. She wanted to see him happy. She wanted to make him happy.

"They're perfect," she told Mr. Rozen.

"Buying presents for the doctors you work with?" a voice asked over her shoulder. Sarah started, then glanced at the woman. Marlena Strange. The model-thin socialite reached out a hand to touch the metal of the cowboy, but Sarah snapped the lid to the box closed, narrowly missing the woman's perfect manicured fingernails.

No way did she want this woman to mar her gifts. "For the men on the ranch." Not that it was any of her business. Marlena and her husband had tried to ruin them earlier in the year. Since then, Sarah knew from her contacts that Marlena had entered therapy for sex addiction and the couple was going for marriage counseling. Sarah had to admire them for trying in a world that seldom bothered. However, she didn't admire the fact the woman had tried to seduce both of her brothers and probably Cal too. Sarah knew her main flaw was a jealous streak that ran a mile wide. She could live with the imperfection.

"Box them up, please," Sarah told the shopkeeper.

"You want to see those earrings again?" Mr. Rozen asked.

"No, I'll just take them. Can I get them all gift-wrapped please?" That would save her precious time. The earrings were for Eliza. Crystal drops on a gold stem. Considering the woman was a gazillionaire it was probably stupid to buy her anything but diamonds. But Sarah knew she'd like them.

She overheard Marlena ask to see the ring in the window and Sarah's mood sank—jealousy, striking again. She paid, then took the bag from the shopkeeper, wishing him a merry Christmas.

She walked outside and was shocked to see Cal standing on the sidewalk frowning at her Explorer. Happiness swelled inside her. She ran toward him and flung her arms around his neck, so glad to see him she kissed him on the mouth, right there on Main Street.

His arms tightened around her for a nanosecond before he stepped out of reach.

Dammit. A wave of hurt rolled through her.

"If I didn't know better, I'd think you were ashamed of me." She tried to keep her voice light, but knew she'd failed when his pupils flared. Apart from that, his expression didn't change. *What the hell?* She wasn't vile, or repulsive. She didn't kick puppies or yell at kids.

Anger replaced the hurt. It was probably the aftereffects of a long day, but she wanted to shock him, to goad him into a reaction. She tried to kiss him again, but he took another half step back, as if she had cooties.

Humiliation flashed hot and painful along her veins. She lost it. On the sidewalk, in the middle of Stone Creek. Totally lost it. "What is the *matter* with you? I've loved you from the moment I first saw you." She was getting louder now, causing a scene. "I never stopped loving you even when you went to prison. I didn't stop loving you when you pretended to think of me as your kid sister." He opened his mouth to argue, but she wasn't done. She was furious. "I love you so much I'm happy to come to your bed every single night, but you won't even acknowledge me when we're off the ranch. How do you think that makes me feel?"

His expression went even more flat as his gaze lifted over her shoulder. *Dammit, he can't even look me in the eye!*

"I never asked you to climb into my bed."

The pain of that statement sent a shockwave through her body. "But you never turned me away, did you?"

His eyes burned into hers suddenly, some of the emotions he kept locked down seeping out. And she wished he'd let go, get angry, get pissed, get even. But he didn't say anything, just grew even more remote. He never revealed anything of himself, except for brief glimpses on the ranch, or when they were in bed and she was wringing a response from him with her body. Hiding emotion was foreign to her. Running around pretending she didn't love this man with every atom of her being seemed fundamentally wrong.

Tears filled her eyes. She'd never learned to be anything other than exactly what she was. *What you see is what you get.* Maybe it wasn't enough for him. Maybe he wanted a different kind of woman and she was being an idiot for throwing herself at him. Even so she put everything on the table. "I want to marry you, Cal. I want to have your babies."

He flinched, his narrowed gaze still directed over her shoulder. He took another step back.

"I'm sorry," he said, very loudly, very clearly. "I don't feel that way about you. I don't love you." Then he walked away and climbed into his truck, which was parked a few cars down from hers. And he drove away without once looking back, as if she really did mean nothing to him.

35

CAL DROVE AROUND the corner and pulled over after a block. He slumped over the steering wheel, sweat making his palms damp. His heart hammered in his chest like a battering ram. The look of devastation on Sarah's face... God, he couldn't stand it. The desire to run back and apologize and make sure she was okay was almost overwhelming.

I want to marry you, Cal. I want to have your babies.

All he'd ever really wanted. Something he'd known for a long time could never be his. He felt sick. She'd just pretty much proposed to him and he'd flat-out rejected her. He scrubbed his hand over his face. He hadn't even done it gently. He'd been too fucking scared.

His stepbrother, Terry, had been standing on the sidewalk behind Sarah, watching them with such malevolence in his eyes it had made Cal's mouth dry up. He clenched his fists. Cal had killed Terry's father— unintentionally, but the result was the same. The younger man had made no secret of the fact he'd happily return the favor to Cal or anyone Cal cared about. The guy was never getting near Sarah.

This was his worst-case scenario. Hopefully his act on the sidewalk would dissuade Terry from doing anything stupid, but Sarah would never forgive Cal for letting her down like that.

A tapping on the glass jerked him back to the present. He looked up and blinked. Sheriff Scott Talbot stood outside his window, hand on gun like he expected Cal to attack him any moment. The man made a twirling motion with his finger. Cal rolled down the window.

"Sheriff. What can I do for you?"

The lawman put on a few pounds of beef lately, and his eyes seemed to get beadier every time they met.

"Step out of the car."

"Can I ask why?"

The sheriff said nothing, just took a wide-stanced step back.

Jesus. Cal kept his face expressionless, but inside he was filled with rage. Making sure his free hand was visible he eased out of the truck. He'd bought the vehicle from Ryan a few months ago. It was old, but the engine was tuned up and ran like a dream. He didn't think there was anything wrong with the taillights or indicators. He made sure to check on a regular basis.

"Up against the vehicle, Landon. You know the drill."

Cal clenched his jaw but held the anger and frustration inside. He "assumed the position." God knew, he'd done it often enough in the past. Ever since he'd gotten out of prison, Talbot stopped him every other week for some perceived infraction or another. The sheriff had eased up some after the shooting at the ranch last spring. But it looked like the vacation was over for Cal. *Merry Christmas.* And Sarah wondered why he didn't want their relationship made public.

"Way you parked up there, I figured maybe you'd imbibed a little too much Christmas spirit down at the saloon."

"No, sir." He'd had a beer while he waited for feed from the hardware store to be ready. One beer.

"Gonna need you to blow into a Breathalyzer for me."

Humiliation rose up inside him. What *he* needed to do was find Sarah and make sure she got home safely. Instead, he took the small black box and blew into that bitch so hard he hoped it'd burst.

The sheriff took it back and squinted at him. "Doesn't look like this thing is working." He shook the unit, as if that would help. Cal rolled his eyes. The reading had been under the legal blood alcohol limit. If he cried police harassment, it'd only get worse.

"Sullivans are gonna need that feed." Cal nodded toward the back of the truck. Snow was forecast by tomorrow. Who knew how long Talbot would detain him. "Better not go missing while you're taking me in and wasting both our time." Pissing off Nat was never a good idea.

"Doing my job isn't wasting time or taxpayers' money, Landon. Sullivans'll get their feed. Don't you worry about that." The guy radioed for assistance so one of his deputies could drive Cal's truck the two blocks to the courthouse. "Let's go down to the sheriff's office and take a blood sample."

CHAPTER FOUR

S ARAH HELD THE steering wheel gripped tight between rigid fingers the whole ten-mile drive home, forcing herself to concentrate on the road and not crash the damned car. Inside she was frozen. Numb. She shook from reaction.

The fact that Cal had said that to her…

She didn't care what other people thought—it was Cal who was hung up on the opinions of others. Sarah didn't give a crap. But he'd said those words out loud for precisely that reason—because *he* cared what others thought, and he didn't want anyone thinking he was involved with her.

When she turned off the main road onto the ranch's drive, she finally allowed tears to blur her vision. She pulled up outside the ranch house and gathered up her things. Her hands shook when they hovered over the boxes of gifts she'd bought, but she stuffed them forcefully inside her purse. There a giant gift-wrapped box containing a doll's house for Tabby, hidden in the trunk. Nat could fetch it later and hide it in the closet, along with all the other presents they'd amassed for the youngest member of the Sullivan family.

She stumbled up the steps, opened the door, walked

through the mudroom, ignoring the dogs, the greetings, the looks of concern when she tossed her bag on the kitchen table and just kept going.

"Sarah?" Nat called. "Sas?" He started following her, moving faster and faster. She wanted to get away, to run, but even though she made it to her room, Nat kept on coming. "What is it? What's wrong?"

His obvious concern tipped her over the edge. She started crying, and he pulled her to his chest and rocked her. He was hot and damp and smelled like horses. More than that, he smelled like safety and security, like her big brother.

"What is it? What happened? Something at work?"

She shook her head. "I'm in love with Cal."

He huffed out a quiet laugh. "Honey, that's hardly news."

She nodded. She might not have said the words, but the truth had always been on her face. "Yeah, well, about a month ago I seduced him."

She heard him grinding his teeth. "Not what I want to think about, but okay. You're an adult, and if you waited for Cal to make a move we'd all be dead."

She started crying harder then, sobbing into his shirt. "He doesn't want me, Nat. I saw him in town and practically begged him to marry me. He told me he didn't want me. Didn't love me."

His arms were banded so tight around her they hurt. "I'm gonna kill him."

She pushed away from him. "He's your best friend, you idiot. You can't kill him just because he doesn't love me back."

Nat's blue eyes widened, then he shook his head. "Not love you back? The guy watches every move you make. He opens your door. Takes your plate at dinner. Polishes your saddle even though you only ride once a month. I'm gonna kill him for being an asshole and making you cry."

Sarah couldn't think straight. She was wiped out, emotionally and physically, and she had another long shift tomorrow. "He loves me like a sister—"

"As your actual brother I can tell you that's *not* how he feels."

"Well, he doesn't love me the way you love Eliza. Or the way Ryan loved Becky. You guys were never ashamed of the person you were with."

Nat sighed. "Cal has some misplaced notion he's not good enough for you—"

"Well grinding me into the dirt is a hell of a way of showing it!"

Nat held up a hand as if to ward off the temper brewing inside her. "I can see this isn't the time to talk about it. Run yourself a hot bath, and I'll bring you up a supper tray." He ran his hand over her bangs, the same thing he did to his horses when their manes got in their eyes. "We'll figure this out. Cal's not going anywhere. You're not going anywhere. He just needs a bit of time to adjust to the fact he's allowed to be happy."

She grabbed his hand. "You don't disapprove?"

Nat gave her an odd look. "Like you said, he's my best friend. Nobody else would be good enough for you."

Sarah nodded, and he left. Inside she still felt hollow and broken. After everything that had happened this year she'd hoped for a good Christmas, a time of joy and new beginnings. But regardless of what Nat thought, maybe she and Cal weren't meant to live happily ever after. Maybe Cal Landon wasn't the man she thought he was.

———————

CAL SAT IN a holding cell trying to ignore the insidious sense of revulsion that crept through every capillary and vein. The memories assaulted him like poison and made him feel sick to his stomach.

He'd been lucky, considering what might have happened to a fourteen-year-old boy in the prison system. Sweat broke out under his shirt and ran down his back. He'd been tried as a juvenile and spent the first four years of his sentence in a juvenile detention center where he'd finished his high school education and figured things weren't so bad. Then he'd been transferred to a men's prison and the shock had almost driven him over the edge. In many ways he'd been lucky there too. He'd been paired with a hard-ass from Idaho called Lloyd Deter. The guy was an anti-government, racist, fascist bigot, but he hadn't been interested in Cal sexually, even though he was fresh meat in a prison population that was only part-human. Lloyd also hadn't wanted anyone defiling his roomie because the idiot seemed to think that being raped by another man would make someone gay, and being gay was apparently contagious. Once the guy assured himself Cal was straight as a hard back chair, he'd protected Cal's ass along with his own. So, yeah, Cal had been lucky. He'd just had to spend years listening to redneck bullshit. And maybe *that* was his real shame. Not being true to himself, to his beliefs. Not standing up for himself in a system where he'd been guaranteed to fail.

He'd got through it. He wasn't proud. Hell, he had nothing to be proud of.

He heard hinges squeak as a door opened and closed down the hall. He looked up. A deputy pushed his stepbrother in front of him toward the holding cell.

Shit. Was this Talbot's twisted Christmas present to Terry?

His stepbrother grinned. Terry had been eight when Cal had killed his daddy. Cal had just wanted the guy to stop hitting his mother. Sadly, Cal's mom had died of a heroin overdose the first year he'd been locked up. Terry had gone to live with some aunt somewhere. Cal figured the kid had been better off.

Terry and his friends had tried to beat him to death in the local roadhouse this past spring. Would have succeeded without Eliza and Nat rescuing his hide. The incident had underlined all the reasons he couldn't afford to let anyone close. He should have left town then, but couldn't bring himself to abandon a family who'd taken him in and loved him like one of their own. Not during their hour of need. When Eliza had been injured and Nat had spent most of his time at the hospital, Cal had picked up the slack. A few months ago, Nat had taken Eliza on a honeymoon to Australia, and Cal had run the ranch with Ryan. But now things had quieted down, they didn't really need him anymore. It might be better all around, especially for Sarah, if he simply left, went somewhere people didn't know about his past, couldn't use it to hurt his friends.

The deputy shot him a steely-eyed stare over Terry's shoulder and then undid the cuffs on his stepbrother's wrists. Then he unlocked Cal's cell door and held it wide.

"I want my lawyer here ASAP," Cal told the deputy. Before he'd been happy to wait out these assholes, but now he was done playing nice.

"Sure thing, Mr. Landon. I'll get right on that." The deputy smirked.

Terry grinned. He wore a tatty leather jacket and liked to think of himself as a biker, but Cal had met real bikers inside and they didn't just ride hogs. They were tough as shit and crossing them was a guaranteed way to get yourself dead. Terry wore the jacket and thought that made him a bad-ass. The guy was a fricking idiot.

The deputy left. Cal figured someone would be watching the video feed and eyed the camera and shook his head. "Been a long time, Terry." He didn't move from where he sat. The other guy walked along the bars until he stood opposite about three feet away.

Terry was younger by six years, skinny and covered in tattoos. "You've been avoiding me, Cal."

Cal let a smile slip. *Not well enough.* "Reckon I have."

Terry took a step forward. "Time's run out." He swung, but Cal ducked.

Cal came to his feet and dodged another fist. "I don't want to fight you, Terry. I know you're pissed. I'd be mad if someone killed my dad, but I never meant to kill him, and I did my time." He might be out of prison, but

44

he paid the price every day of his whole life, and regretted his actions more than he could ever say.

Terry swung again and connected with his cheek. Cal gave him that one.

"You fucking asshole. Did your time? You killed my father! He was a good man."

Cal avoided another punch and backed away, hands in the air. "He was an abusive dickwad. If I hadn't stopped him, he'd have killed my mom and probably us too."

"Your mother was a crack whore!" Terry screamed.

And that made it okay?

Terry's mother had died in a car wreck where Terry's father had been driving. He was never charged, but everyone knew he'd been drunk at the wheel. He was no angel. Cal's mother had attached herself to the single dad, and they'd gotten married shortly after. A match made in hell. They'd barely made it through the wedding ceremony before the guy started beating her.

Cal danced away. He'd already inflicted too much damage on the other man. He had no desire to ever commit a violent act again, but as Terry started laying into his stomach, Cal suddenly had enough. Enough of apologizing every day of his life. Enough of being the doormat that the cops wiped their feet on. He was lean, but it was all muscle, and he'd learned to fight in the big house. He ducked away and danced on his toes. Terry swung at him and swiped air. Cal laughed.

Terry's eyes grew small and mean. "Gonna go find that cute little blonde with the fine ass when I get outta here." He cupped his crotch. "Give her a taste of what a real man can offer her."

Cal punched Terry in the nose and heard it crack. Then he jabbed him again in the mouth, watched as Terry's head snapped back and used a one-two to drop him to the cement floor. He stood, breathing hard, as the guy lay there coughing on the floor.

"Go near that *girl* or even look at her ass, and I will make you wish you died the same day as your daddy. Got it?" He moved away as the deputies finally rushed in. He stood shaking his head as one of them smacked him hard enough against the bars so his nose gushed with blood. Like he'd ever want to drag a woman like Sarah into the dregs of his world. He spat out blood. *Damn.* It was gonna be a long night.

CHAPTER FIVE

C AL PULLED UP outside the horse barn. It was eight in the morning and he'd spent the whole night sitting in a stinking jail cell, worried that as soon as Terry got out he'd gone hunting for Sarah. Cal had passed her on the drive home, and she was already on her way to work. She'd assiduously avoided eye contact.

Cal had been released without charge as soon as his court-appointed lawyer turned up. Apparently the sheriff hadn't called her until six o'clock this morning—a "communications error" according to Talbot. The lawyer—a young lady named Deanna Montrose—had urged Cal to file an official complaint, but he'd just wanted to get out of there and make sure Sarah was okay. He'd phoned to apologize and tell her to watch out for his stepbrother, but she wasn't answering her cell. He'd hurt her yesterday and the look in her eyes when he'd lied and said he didn't love her? It gutted him. But maybe it was for the best.

He dragged the first sack of feed off the bed of the truck, hoisted it over his shoulder. Did the same with a second bag. He turned and there stood Nat, staring at him with a wariness in his eyes he'd never seen before.

"What happened?" asked Nat.

"I got held up in town."

"You go get drunk after you upset my sister?"

Cal narrowed his gaze. "*Yeah*, that's what I did."

Nat knew him better than that. He must have caught sight of the blood on his collar, or maybe the exhaustion in his eyes, and let it go. He grabbed two sacks out of the back of the trunk. "Snow's coming."

Cal looked up at the sky and saw the heaviness in the clouds. He didn't mind winter. Some days he wished they'd get snowed in forever. "Yup." He went inside the horse barn and dumped the bag in the feed room.

Nat followed him, blocked his way out. "She cried all night—right up until she snuck out to go to your cabin only to discover you never came home last night."

Cal closed his eyes and leaned his forehead against the cold wall. "I never wanted to hurt her."

"Why are you then?" asked Nat.

He clamped his jaws together, refusing to talk about it.

"Figure it the fuck out," Nat bit out. They went back out to the truck to haul more supplies. "She's loved you since you first came out here that summer before we started high school."

Cal swallowed and nodded. It had been the best summer of his life. Even having the twins follow them everywhere had been kind of cute. He'd seen a real family in action that summer, learned the value of hard work, and discovered he liked it. Nat had stood by him during the trial and afterward. Nat's father, Jake, had even vouched for his character in court which had helped reduce his sentence. Cal owed these people everything, and right now was doing nothing but causing them trouble.

"She's my kid sister." Nat pushed his hat to the back of his head. "I can't stand to see her hurting. Not when she's been through so much. Not when I know how you feel about her."

Cal made a decision. It would be like driving nails through his skull, but he was doing it. He was leaving the Triple H and a woman who could have any man she wanted.

A huge ball of emotion clogged his throat. After a few months she'd forget all about him.

"Gotta go feed the horses." He turned his back on his best friend and fought a surge of emotion that made him want to weep. He wanted to stay here. With every cell in his body he wanted to be part of this family, to love Sarah and raise babies together. But he'd seen how easy it was to hurt a woman. He knew Eliza had already suffered brutality at the hands of another man. He couldn't increase the danger they faced. No man worth his salt would bring trouble to good people.

The only thing he could do to guarantee their safety was to leave.

———

CAL HADN'T COME home last night. Sarah ground her teeth. When she'd passed him on the highway he'd been wearing the same shirt he'd had on yesterday. She could only assume he'd slept in the truck rather than be anywhere near her, or gotten blind drunk, or—her heart gave a squeeze—spent the night with some other woman just to prove how little she meant to him.

To think she'd gone to the cabin, swallowed her pride, determined to talk—and knew with a feeling of shame that she'd have settled for sex just to feel close to him, just to feel like they weren't actually over.

God.

She was pathetic.

Love *sucked*.

She pulled up in the parking lot of the hospital, forced a cheery voice as she spoke to the three-year-old cherub in the rear seat. "Here we are. Is Santa coming to daycare today, Tabby?"

The little blonde girl quivered with excitement. She'd just begun to understand what Christmas was all about and was hitting the holiday fueled with anticipation, excitement and an overdose of silver glitter. Sarah climbed out of the car and opened the back door to unclip Tabby from her car seat. She lifted the little girl down. Tabby looked so cute in her pink boots, tights and dress. She wore a white jacket with a fur collar and looked so much like her mother it brought a vicious ache to Sarah's throat. She should stop feeling sorry for herself. Her love life was a train wreck, but so what? Becky had been her best friend in high school. At some point, the other girl had started spending as much time with Ryan as she had with Sarah and, although she'd been a little slow on the uptake, Sarah had eventually figured they were an item and she was the third wheel. Becky and Ryan had dated throughout the rest of high school and then they'd both attended Montana State.

They'd gotten married the summer after graduation and Sarah swore she'd never seen two people happier or more suited. The wedding had been perfect. Their lives together had been perfect. The only time she'd seen them fight was when Becky was diagnosed with breast cancer. She'd been pregnant with Tabitha and had refused treatment until the baby was born, but by then it was too late. She'd died not long after she'd first held Tabitha in her arms, and Sarah had thought for a long time she was going to lose her brother too. Ryan had never really gotten over it, but he seemed to have pulled back from the brink of self-destruction. He was finally beginning to get to know his daughter, but Sarah knew he remained heartbroken.

She'd ached for him. Mourned with him. And done her best to fill in for a mother who had loved her little girl with her whole being. Sarah had made it her quest to fill Tabby's life with the happy memories all kids deserved. It was the least she could do. She grabbed her medical bag and Tabitha's lunch box, and they held hands as they headed to the daycare attached to the hospital.

Looking after this beautiful little girl helped take her mind off her bruised feelings.

Sarah led Tabby through the long corridor and pressed the buzzer to get into the daycare. It was supposed to be staff children only, but they'd made special dispensation for her. Good job considering the shortage of doctors they'd had lately.

They had a new Attending Physician starting on Christmas Day, poor soul. And as soon as Sarah finalized plans with the local family practitioner in Stone Creek, they were going to have to find themselves another resident.

She kissed Tabitha goodbye, promising to pick her up at four sharp so they could get back in time for a big family supper. She'd see Cal then. They'd talk. Another wave of emotion hit. Maybe it would do them good to have a few hours apart. Time to cool off. To think about whether or not they had a future together as a couple.

Just because she loved him didn't mean she was blind to his faults. Life wasn't all flowers and love songs—and come to think of it, most love songs ended in a bitter twist.

She put her jacket and bag in her locker, pulled on her white coat and slung her stethoscope around her neck, took a deep breath. *Here goes.* She pushed through the doors, and into chaos.

Five miles beyond Stone Creek, County Hospital served a town of about fifteen thousand and a large, mainly rural community. They saw everything from dismemberment via farm equipment, gunshot wounds, car accidents, and the usual daily quota of aches, pains, fevers and childhood injuries.

She wanted to be busy. She needed the distraction. "Who've we got up first, Madge?" she asked the charge nurse.

"Mrs. Henriksson in exam one, Dr. Sullivan. May I say how very attractive you look today, girl? Is that for the benefit of our hot new orthopedic surgeon?"

Sarah shot Madge a wry look. She'd worn the red wraparound dress with her tall black boots as a way of bolstering her deflated spirits. She'd forgotten she was avoiding the attention of one Reilly Spencer. She stuck her tongue out at the nurse she'd known for years. "Warn me if you see him," she whispered.

"See who?" A deep voice spoke from behind her.

Sarah whirled. *Crap.* "Just a patient. How're you settling in, Dr. Spencer?"

His eyes ran down her red dress before skipping back to her face. The guy looked genuinely interested. Considering she'd cried half the night and hadn't slept a wink, she was surprised he didn't run screaming through the big double doors. He squeezed her arm in an overly familiar gesture, and his warm breath stroked her ear as he leaned in. "Let me know if you need any help."

"I will, thanks." She moved away and shot Madge a glare over her other shoulder. She could imagine the nonsense the senior ER nurse was filling his head with. *Hasn't had a date in years. Dedicated to her work and her family. Drudge.* Blah. Blah. How about getting hot and heavy with a very fine cowboy every night for the last several weeks, huh?

Her mood slumped.

She was off men. Definitely off cowboys.

She whipped through the curtain to exam one. "Mrs. Henriksson…" *Whoa, holy moly.* She assessed her patient's face. One big purple contusion, topped with a broken nose. Sarah cleared her throat as she read the chart. "Can you tell me what happened?"

Heather Henriksson raised a hand to her forehead in a self-conscious gesture. "I walked into a door."

Sarah raised her brow, not in the mood for bullshit.

"Did the door have fists?"

The woman looked away. Sarah noticed a small boy sitting on the floor beside the bed. He was maybe five. Wearing Spiderman pajamas. Crap.

"Hey, Buddy, what's your name?"

The child looked down at the floor, and his mom reached out her hand. "This is Henry Junior."

The almost desperate grip the mother kept on her son sent a little tug to Sarah's heart. "And who brought you in, Mrs. Henriksson?"

The woman coughed and immediately hugged her ribs. "My husband dropped me off. He had to go run some Christmas errands."

Making up for beating the shit out of his wife by buying a few presents and groceries? Or too ashamed to show his face?

"Do you have a headache?" Sarah asked. How could she not? Sarah had a headache just looking at her.

"My head hurts, yes." Mrs. Henriksson touched her forehead.

Sarah examined her while the boy watched with big brown eyes. He made her think of Cal and everything he'd endured growing up. Dammit, no wonder he struggled with relationships. "Mrs. Henriksson, Heather, I'm worried you might have a broken rib and be concussed. We're going to send you for chest X-rays and a CT scan. Is there someone who could watch Henry Junior for you?" Sarah pointed toward the little boy who tried to slide under the bed so he wouldn't get noticed. How different he was to Tabitha, who strutted her pink glory like royalty. This kid wanted to be wallpaper. Her

54

heart started to break. Then she started to get pissed.

"I want to keep him with me," Heather Henriksson insisted.

"You don't want me to call your husband?" said Sarah without inflection.

Eyes that were almost swollen shut flashed in alarm. She carefully shook her head. Sarah sat on the bed and took the woman's free hand. She kept her voice low. "If your husband did this to you, Heather, you have to report him. You have to get out of that house before he kills you or your son."

For a moment Sarah thought she was getting through to the woman. The opportunity was shattered when a deep male voice spoke from the other side of the curtain. Heather flinched away and the kid pretty much crawled under the bed as the curtain was flung back.

Henry Henriksson was a big man, with thick heavy shoulders, and a good-looking face. His eyes ran over their joined hands. Heather pulled hers sharply from Sarah's grip.

"Mr. Henriksson?" Sarah stood and offered her hand to the man with a smile. She should be an actress. The top of her head came to his mid chest, but she wasn't intimidated. "I'm Dr. Sullivan."

The big man took Sarah's tiny hand in his. She held on when he went to withdraw, and she turned his damaged knuckles to the light. "Ouch. Those injuries look sore, Mr. Henriksson. Would you like me to dress them?" She kept her eyes wide and her expression blank, but he knew she knew exactly what he'd done.

His gaze narrowed, and he dropped her hand. "Let's

go," he told the woman in the bed.

"We're not ready to release Mrs. Henriksson, yet." Sarah made it a statement, not an option. "Your wife might have a concussion, and I think at least one of her ribs is broken. It's going to take a few hours to run tests."

The man shifted his weight from foot to foot, expression hard, lips drawn. If he attacked her, it would hurt, but Sarah did not move from her position in front of the injured woman. It wasn't bravery. Sarah had always had people to stand up for her—her parents, her brothers, Cal, heck, even hospital security. This woman had no one. "I suggest you come back around noon and see where we're at. It'll give you the chance to finish the Christmas preparations and your wife a chance to rest. I'm sure you wouldn't want another wasted journey or for Heather to have to be readmitted in a few hours' time." *Not to mention ending up on a murder charge should this defenseless woman die from a brain bleed you caused, you sick mofo.*

The man looked foiled. Then he caught sight of his son. He jerked his head. "Henry Junior, come with me. We'll be back in a few hours and see how your mama is getting on." The woman on the bed started to sit upright. Any moment now, she was going to declare herself "fine" and sign herself out of the hospital.

"I asked Henry Junior if he wanted to meet Santa who's visiting some of the wards today. It's no bother for him to stay and play with the other children, if that's okay with you?" Sarah smiled at the little boy. She really should have gone into acting.

"I'll make sure they are finished by noon, honey."

Heather Henriksson's voice was so sweet it made Sarah want to puke. "Sorry to mess up your day like this."

Sarah hid her disgust. *Sorry I need medical attention because you hit a woman half your size so hard your fists bled. And so sorry I broke my ribs on your poor bruised hands.* At least he hadn't turned his fury on their precious child.

Sarah knew the drill. She'd seen it often enough in the past. She wanted to get this woman out of an abusive situation, but the chances of that happening were slim. Women, and sometimes men, were trapped in circumstances and a cycle of abuse. They couldn't see the way out. Some were too scared to leave. Some didn't think they deserved help. How a human being believed they deserved such treatment was beyond her. They wouldn't treat an animal this poorly.

She didn't get it. She would never get it.

Silence stretched taut. She braced herself. She knew exactly where he'd be spending Christmas if he laid a hand on her, and she relished the thought. Still, she didn't want to make the situation worse for Heather and the little boy, because chances were they would go home eventually.

He took a step back, checked his wristwatch. Sarah's shoulders sagged.

"I'll be back at noon." He turned his eyes on his wife. "Make sure you're down here waiting for me." His tone brooked no refusal. Heather nodded.

Sarah blew out a big breath as he walked away. She turned back to the woman. "I'm going to take Henry Junior to spend a couple hours in the daycare while you have your tests done." Heather opened her mouth to argue, but Sarah took her hand and squeezed. "He'll be safe, and he'll have fun. It'll be good for him. Trust me."

The woman finally nodded and Sarah leaned closer. "There are people who can help you, Heather. Places you can go."

Heather bit her lip, then clutched harder at her hand. "I'm pregnant."

Sarah almost reared back in shock. "Does he know?"

Heather's face crumpled, and she started to cry. She nodded. "He was angry about it. Said we can't afford another mouth to feed." She gave a wet sniffle. "Will you make sure my baby is okay?"

Tears filled Sarah's eyes. What was wrong with the world?

It was Christmas. Sarah was determined to make something good happen today. "Okay, Henry Junior. Let's go see Santa." She held out her hand and, after a slight hesitation, the little boy took it. She looked at the mom. "I'm sending you for a head CT first, then we'll see about the baby, all right?"

The woman nodded, but misery dragged at her features. "Be a good boy, Henry Junior."

Sarah would bet the ranch little Henry Junior was *always* a good boy. It wouldn't keep him safe though. Eventually those fists would lash out in his direction. If he was lucky, he'd end up like Cal. If he was unlucky, he'd end up dead. And to think she'd been feeling sorry for herself this morning.

What an idiot.

NAT AND ELIZA had gone to buy groceries to last through next week. Ezra was visiting his new lady friend—apparently even men with no teeth had a better love life than Cal did. And Ryan was checking cattle in one of the upper pastures. The house was empty of people but full of memories. It was the only true home he'd ever known. Cal had fed the horses, written Sarah, Nat, and Ryan a short letter each and put them on the mantel.

He'd thrown his gear in a kit bag and stood looking at the pale blue-gray of the jagged mountains that surrounded them. He was never going to forget this place. Even the air here seemed different. Clean, fresh, brilliant. Cal wouldn't have considered himself fanciful, but this land held magic—from the eagles soaring over the highest peaks, to the tiny flowers that hid among the damp hemlock groves. He pressed his lips together and gave the ranch dog one last scratch on the neck. The old dog's back leg started moving in appreciation.

Cal got in his truck and drove away, looking at the L-frame ranch house in the rearview the entire drive out.

It might be better this way, but the idea of leaving ripped out his heart. And that emotion paled beside the idea of not seeing Sarah ever again. She was going to be so upset to get that damned letter. What sort of jerk broke things off with a letter? Especially at Christmas? His fingers gripped the steering wheel. He'd told himself it was better for her if he just walked away, but that was pure cowardice talking. He was too scared to face her.

He'd known her for more than two decades and loved her so much he felt like he was drowning in it. But Terry's warning echoed inside his head. The threat was very real.

But sneaking off like a coward was not going to fly. So rather than turning the wheel left, away from town, he turned it right. He needed to look Sarah in the eye when he said goodbye. Tell her exactly why he was going. He didn't want her to think even for a minute he didn't love and respect her. Hell, he cared for her more than anyone and would sacrifice every last person on the planet to keep her safe. She didn't need to know *that*, but she did need to know she deserved better than a bum like him.

The flashing lights took him by surprise. He glanced at his speedometer and realized he'd been so distracted by the idea of going to Sarah, he'd gone ten miles over the speed limit along the straight road that led into town. As Sheriff Talbot climbed out of his cruiser, Cal started laughing. The guy had finally nailed him for something legit. Son of a bitch.

CHAPTER SIX

S ARAH BARELY HAD time to think following a road traffic accident that brought in three trauma patients, two in critical condition. She'd sent the third teenager up to X-ray after helping wrap a cast from his wrist to his shoulder, and a matching one on his leg. He was the lucky one.

She grabbed a coffee from the break room and walked over to the desk to see where they were in the war against the daily madness. She glanced left and saw Henry Henriksson talking to Sheila Goldstein in the corridor.

Crap. "Who called Child Services?" Sarah asked Madge. She'd debated and decided to try to talk Heather into filing a police report first. Then she'd forgotten all about the Henrikssons while fighting to save the life of someone's teenage daughter. She needed a clone.

"Dr. Spencer alerted social services, and they called in Sheila."

"I want my son back." Henriksson's voice rose over the noise of the waiting room. "And I want my wife down here, right now." He looked up and caught Sarah's eye. "You lied to me, bitch." His gaze narrowed into pure hatred, and her heart knocked against her ribs. People glanced toward her nervously. Then security stepped in with Sheila trying to explain protocol to the enraged man. He flung off the hands of the security personnel, turned on his heel, and strode outside.

Madge put her palm on her chest. "Lord have mercy, I thought he was about to lose his shit right here."

She nodded. "Me too. Who's next?" Some people had been here for hours. She went through charts with Madge, trying to figure out who needed her most.

There was a strange ratcheting noise at the entrance. When Sarah looked across to the front door, every drop of blood drained from her head. Henriksson had come back inside, only this time he was carrying a rifle.

Sarah didn't think. She ran. She had to find Henriksson's wife and son before he did. She ran around the corner and heard gunfire as she dove into the elevator and slapped the button. A bullet dinged the metal interior just as the door closed. The guy had stepped over a line he could never come back from. She headed to level three even though Heather Henriksson was on four. She silently apologized to everyone on that floor as she got off and shouted to the staff, "Armed intruder! Lock this floor down immediately!"

She hit the stairs and started pounding up the concrete steps. She burst onto the fourth floor and fled along the corridor, shouting the same message. People scattered and started shutting down the elevator and securing fire doors, getting patients back to their beds and barricading themselves inside. Sarah ran into the room where they conducted the CT scans.

"Where's Heather Henriksson?" she asked.

The technician climbed uncertainly to her feet. "She left. Said she was going to get her son and go home."

A wave of terror shot through her. Oh, God. The daycare. She had to make sure the children were safe. But the alarm had been raised, and they would shut the place down. She knew that, but it didn't make her worry any less. She grabbed her phone out of her pocket, texted Nat to get to Tabitha ASAP. He'd called earlier to say he and Eliza were in town. She stood there panting. *Okay—think rationally for a moment.* Doors into the wards were locked. The guy might be trapped inside the elevator for all she knew. The cops would be here soon, and Mr. Henriksson would be detained.

Reilly Spencer came running out of his office. It looked as if he'd been catching a quick nap. "What's going on?" he asked.

"That guy you called social services on?" The sound of gunfire permeated the air again, sending a quiver of fear through her bones. "Let's just say he wasn't very happy about it."

Spencer's eyes widened. "Oh, shit. The place is secure, right?"

Sarah breathed out a lungful of terror. "As locked down as a place this size can be."

Then her heart started hammering as a noise that could only be the service elevator started to rumble. She grabbed keys from the nurse's desk and ran for the fire exit. "Get into your offices and lock the doors." She undid the fire door, which the staff had secured.

"What are you going to do?" Spencer asked, hovering uncertainly.

Her hands shook as she got the door open. "Draw him away from patients. I'm the one who spoke to him this morning, and he's blaming me for getting social services involved. I promised him his wife would be ready to go at noon, and he thinks I set this whole thing up." Spencer ran toward her. There was no time to argue with him as the service elevator opened and out stepped Henry Henriksson. His eyes found her, and he raised the rifle to his shoulder just as Dr. Spencer slid through the open fire door and Sarah slammed it shut behind him. They both started running.

"Why are we going up?" Spencer demanded, breathing heavily.

"You're going to warn the pediatric ward and make sure they are barricaded inside. I'm going to the roof and down the fire escape ladder. Then I'll head to the daycare. I need to find Henriksson's wife and son." And Tabitha.

What sort of world did they live in where a man could beat his wife, then threaten anyone who objected with a gun? The echo of footsteps below them had them both running faster.

———

CAL HANDED OVER his insurance and registration.

Talbot was grinning at him like a man who'd won a full million on the lottery.

"Surely you have better things to do on Christmas Eve?" Cal asked the guy.

"Despite what you may think, I don't sit around

waiting for you to screw up, Landon." The sheriff's expression grew grim. "There was an accident on the sixty-eight, and I was just heading back to town when I saw someone speeding. Not my fault you were breaking the law."

"Was the accident bad?" Cal asked. Shit. What a thing to happen on Christmas Eve.

The sheriff looked down at his feet. "Three teenagers driving too fast, ran off the road and rolled a bunch of times." He hitched up his equipment belt.

Cal winced. The guy was a dick, but Cal didn't envy him his job. "Well, I hope they're okay."

The radio went off, and the sheriff froze in the act of writing out his ticket. He reached down. "Repeat dispatch."

Cal heard "man with a gun" and "shots fired" and then the location, "County Hospital." A very bad feeling came over him.

"Ten-four. I'm en route." Talbot threw Cal's documents back at him through the open window. "Consider this a warning." He jogged back to his car, put on the sirens and cherry lights, and took off.

What the hell? Cal frowned. *A shooter at County?*

He put his truck in gear and pressed his foot down to the floor. He tried to call Sarah on her cell, but she didn't answer. Dammit. He called Nat instead. "Something's going on at County. Meet me there soon as you can."

He turned on the radio, and a chill rushed over his body. Reports of an armed intruder and shots fired *inside* the hospital. He called Ryan, but despite Eliza's high-tech upgrades, cell reception was always spotty and inconsistent on the ranch. He left a message.

Seconds seemed to last forever as he drove the remaining miles to the hospital, foot pressed to the boards most of the way. The sight of Sarah's Explorer in the parking lot sent a fresh bolt of panic through his veins, as did the sight of black-clad cops surrounding the front entrance. Sarah was in there somewhere. And Tabitha.

A tap on his shoulder had him whirling.

"Is Sarah here?" It was Eliza. Nat stood behind her, eyes scanning the milling crowd that the cops were trying to force back.

Cal swallowed his fear. Shook his head. "Radio said an armed intruder was in the building."

"Sarah texted me to come get Tabitha." Even as Nat spoke Cal saw a stream of children being led to safety off to the right. "Eliza, would you please go find Tabitha and look after her until Ryan arrives, *please*?" The inflection in his voice begged her to do as he asked.

She nodded. Then she slipped something into Nat's hand and pulled his jacket closed to hide it. Her Glock. "I'm going to make sure Tabitha is safe and see what else I can find out. I don't want either of you to get hurt, but I have about as much faith in the local cops as in a group of high school students paintballing."

Nat's cell beeped again. He checked it. "Sarah's headed to the roof."

Eliza nodded. She'd spent weeks here in the spring. "There's a fire escape around the back of the building that leads from the roof to the ground floor. Go get her to safety, but *don't* get shot." Her gaze was fierce as she kissed her husband full on the lips. Then she cupped

Cal's jaw and gave him a quick smile. "And if you don't treat her right when we get her out of there, I'm going to shoot you myself." She shook her head at him and walked away.

Cal watched her leave. If anyone understood exactly what was going on inside his brain, it was Eliza. And he had the sudden realization that running away to keep others safe hadn't seemed any more reasonable when she'd tried it either.

———

SPENCER REILLY PEELED off on the top floor of the building and ran into the pediatric ward, locking the door behind him. She heard him shouting instructions to the people inside. Henriksson was panting heavily in their wake.

"I want my wife back, you lying bitch!" he screamed at her.

Great. The slurred words suggested he'd used the morning to refuel his anger with whiskey.

An armed, drunk, wife-beater on Christmas. What could possibly go wrong?

She hit the roof level and said a huge "thank you" to the man upstairs when the door opened easily. She slammed it shut and used the master key to lock it behind her. She needed to buy enough time to get down the fire escape. Hopefully local cops would be in the stairwell making their way up. If they could trap the man there, maybe they could talk him down and no one would get hurt. She ran over to the metal ladder and peered down the five stories, swaying slightly as vertigo hit her. Heights were not her thing.

No time to think. Even over the wind she heard Henriksson pounding on the door. She swung her leg over onto the fire escape and gripped the frigid metal with both hands. The rat-tat-tat of automatic gunfire had her shaking in fear. As fast as she dared, she descended, rust staining her hands orange as the wind whipped up her dress. She shook from cold and fear, her grip getting weaker as she moved as quickly as she could, desperate for the relative safety of the first landing. Suddenly she was looking along the barrel of a rifle, followed by the angry face of Henry Henriksson as he stared over the parapet.

"Get your ass back up here, bitch, or I'll shoot you where you are." His fingers tightened on the trigger and Sarah knew, if she wanted to live, she had to stop running. *Dammit.* She swallowed and nodded. The chances of making it out of this situation alive had just plummeted.

CAL SPRINTED WITH Nat on his heels. The local cops were concentrating on the front of the building and people were pouring out, white-faced with fear. The police didn't have enough manpower to search the entire hospital, control the crowd, segregate potential bad guys, targets, and innocent bystanders. Trying to locate one doctor in this crazy melee would not be their priority. But it was his. He jumped a low wall and smashed through the shrubbery, slamming to a stop with his arm across Nat's chest as a flash of color high above them caught his eye. Cal's brain felt as if someone had plugged him into the mains as he watched a man grab a small blonde figure in a red dress and haul her back onto the roof.

"What was Sarah wearing when she left for work this morning?" he asked.

Nat's mouth was a stern line. "A red dress. Let's go."

As soon as the son of a bitch with the rifle moved away from the wall, Cal ran to the fire escape, leaped the first eight feet to the first rung, and hauled himself up, then started climbing fast. The ladder was noisy, but Cal hoped the wind whipped the sound away. After a few more rungs, he toed off his boots. Nat swore as one hit him, but Cal was able to move with much more stealth in his socks. The ladder squeaked slightly but didn't groan as he raced up the metal skeleton. When he got to the top, he glanced around but didn't see any sign of the attacker. He jumped over the ledge and waited for Nat to join him. Nat's bare feet should have made him smile, but he was too numb inside. He grabbed Nat's arm, pulled him close enough to whisper in his ear.

The guy needed to know the truth before they got into this. "My stepbrother, Terry, threatened Sarah yesterday. That's why I pushed her away and told her I didn't love her. He was standing right behind her at the time." He'd never forgive himself if Sarah was hurt.

Nat's eyes flashed. "Terry is an asshole, but this isn't about him. I recognize the guy with the rifle. Henry Henriksson. I'm guessing he finally put his wife in the hospital and got a little upset when someone reported him."

Cal's heart raced. "So this isn't because of Terry?"

Nat shook his head.

Cal couldn't believe how convinced he'd been that this was all his fault. It steadied him, though in reality, it made no difference. Sarah was still in imminent danger from a misogynist. The idea of anyone laying hands on her…

Nat pulled out Eliza's Glock and checked the witness hole. There was a bullet in the chamber.

Cal was unarmed, but that didn't mean he wasn't dangerous. If the guy hurt Sarah he was going to throw him right off the damned roof. "I'll circle around the back of the ventilation stack. See if he's there."

Nat nodded. "I'm going to head west. We'll meet on the other side of the stairwell." Nat pulled out his cell. "Switch yours to silent. Let's keep an open line between us so we can hear what's going on—I'll add Eliza to the call too. Hopefully she can stop the cops from shooting us."

It might stop them shooting Nat, but Cal didn't think it would win him any favors. He nodded and did as Nat suggested, holding the phone to his ear as he moved cautiously from one piece of cover to the next. There was no one near the ventilation stack.

He heard voices and made his way carefully toward the far side of the stairwell.

"Tell me where my wife and child are, you fucking bitch!" Henriksson shouted at Sarah.

Cal edged around the corner and saw a man holding

Sarah by the hair, her face twisted in pain. He wanted to charge the guy, but the barrel was pointed at Sarah's body in a one handed grip. If Cal surprised the bastard, it would be all too easy for him to pull the trigger.

Cal didn't recognize him and doubted Henriksson knew his connection to Sarah or the Sullivans. He figured he could draw him out.

He put the phone to his ear and wandered casually into sight. He let his eyes widen in horror as both Henriksson and Sarah looked at him with matching expressions of surprise.

Cal raised his hands and slipped the cell into his shirt pocket. "Dude," he said, hoping Sarah played along. "What's going on, man?"

"Who the fuck are you?"

Cal took a step back. Henriksson pushed Sarah out of the door as if to follow him. *Come on, buddy. Come to Papa.* Nat was an excellent shot. Cal just had to get Henriksson into the open and Sarah away from that damned rifle barrel.

"I came up for a quiet smoke," said Cal. He hoped to hell the guy didn't notice his lack of shoes.

Sarah hid her reaction to his appearance with a squirm that Cal prayed wouldn't earn her a bullet.

"Mr. Henriksson here is looking for his wife." Sarah's eyes spat defiance. "I told him his wife discharged herself and is probably on her way home with their son, right now, but he doesn't believe me."

Henriksson tightened his grip on Sarah's hair and she cried out. Cal had to clamp down on the desire to pummel the bastard to death for laying a hand on his woman. Instead he took a step back, and the guy lumbered toward him. "Dude. This isn't cool. Let the doc go, and go find your wife. Your missus isn't up on the roof, that's for darn sure." He guffawed like an idiot and drew the guy out another step. *Come on, asshole.*

Henriksson jabbed Sarah hard in the ribs. "She set social services on me. I'm gonna give her a reason why bitches should keep their big mouths shut."

"Hey, man, I get it." Cal sent a silent apology to women everywhere. "Some bitches deserve what they get." He let his voice get hard, and Sarah's brows rose to her hairline. But finally Henriksson was out in the open and Cal watched Nat slip around the door until he was standing a few feet behind the guy. Henriksson was even bigger than Nat. Hell, the guy probably weighed the same as the two of them put together.

Cal waited for Nat to strike the butt of his weapon into the gunman's temple. But even then, Henriksson didn't go down. Instead, he gave a bear-like bellow and twisted violently, Sarah and the gun both still in his grip. Cal grabbed the gun, shoving the barrel until it pointed into the air. Henriksson pulled the trigger and Cal held on, the barrel burning his fingers as it jerked in his hands. He drove his knee into the big man's balls while Nat dragged Sarah out of harm's way and pushed her behind him, into the stairwell.

"Run, Sarah!" Cal shouted. "Get out of here."

Henriksson changed tactics and drove forward, pushing Cal backward. *Oh, shit.* They gained momentum. The lunatic was going to drive him right off the edge of the building. Cal shoved his legs between the other man's and hooked his foot around his knee. Henriksson tripped and landed like a beached whale on top of Cal. The gun went off again. The noise deafening in intensity, bullets pinging off the brickwork. His eyes searched for Sarah, but he couldn't see her, thank God. Then Henriksson pressed his forearm across Cal's throat and Cal couldn't breathe. He couldn't defend himself without letting go of the rifle barrel, and if he did that, he was dead. Instead, he helped the asshole empty the magazine, praying the ricochets wouldn't kill him as his eardrums threatened to burst from the noise. His vision started to gray, but he remembered his legs. He brought his knees hard into Henriksson's kidney although they didn't seem to have an impact. The gun finally clicked without firing. Empty.

Cal smiled. Now they were even.

He pried one arm loose and clawed at the giant's eye, digging his short nails deep into the socket. Nat was behind him trying to draw a bead, but right now they were so tangled up it was impossible to shoot Henriksson without nailing Cal.

Cal dug his fingers in harder. Henriksson reared back in pain, taking the pressure off Cal's throat and letting him catch a breath.

"Stop or I'll shoot," Nat called.

Henriksson rolled, dragging Cal to his feet, holding him like a shield in front of him. The man threw down his empty weapon. Sarah ran out of hiding and stood beside Nat, love for Cal shining clear in her eyes. The big man literally carried him backward, toward the drop-off that would kill them both. All Cal could think was he'd never said the words. He'd never told Sarah he loved her.

The knowledge spurred him on. He hadn't defended himself and his mother all those years ago just so he could die at the hands of another abusive bastard.

He drove his elbow hard into Henriksson's gut. Then smashed his fist backward into the man's nose, driving the cartilage upward into his skull. Henriksson stumbled on the very edge of the building. Cal went down hard to his knees, but the big guy had too much momentum, and was too close to the edge. His arms windmilled and he started falling. *Dammit*. Part of Cal wanted to let him go, let him fall, and eliminate the problem. But he couldn't. Cal lunged forward and grabbed Henriksson's hand. He heard the rush of feet behind him as Nat leaped to do the same. And suddenly there they were, holding onto the fucking asshole as he dangled off the hospital roof.

"Don't let me fall. *Please* don't let me fall," Henriksson begged.

"I'm tempted to just let him go," Nat deadpanned. "World would be a better place."

They let the words sit there for a moment, small revenge for the panic and fear this man had caused on a day that should have been filled with nothing but joy and peace.

"No," Cal said clearly. He knew what he wanted now. He'd finally figured out bad things sometimes happened whether he was around or not. At least if he stuck close, he could watch out for the people he loved, rather than running away like a dumbass. "I want him to answer for laying hands on *my* woman. I want him to find out what the prison population does to a big man who beats up women." His arms felt like they were being pulled from their sockets. Christ, if someone didn't help soon they were going to drop the bastard whether they wanted to or not. Finally, Cal heard the sounds of booted feet. Other hands reached out and hauled Henriksson over the top of the wall, and dragged him farther onto the roof, before cuffing him.

Cal rolled away from the edge and stared up at the pewter sky. Suddenly, Sarah was standing over him. Hands on her hips, looking like a dream come true. Tall black boots, and a red dress that clung to every curve and had come a little askew in the tussle. His eyes traveled up her legs. Even in her white coat she looked hot. Dear God, he was lying there surrounded by twenty law enforcement officers and getting a hard-on just looking at her.

"Forgive me?" he asked quietly.

She looked like she wanted to tap her foot. "Ready to go public with our relationship yet, Landon?"

He came up onto his knees, looked around at a couple of deputies who'd probably break out the cuffs on him next. They were grinning. He looked back at Sarah. "Reckon I just did." Then he grabbed her hand and pulled her down beside him. Rolled her so she was lying beneath him. He brushed her hair away from her face. "I love you, Sarah Sullivan." He kissed her slowly and tenderly, relishing the contact. "You deserve someone a million times better than me, but if you really want me, let's get married."

She smiled at him then, but her eyes narrowed.

Uh oh.

"*Let's get married?*" Her brows climbed sky-high. He obviously wasn't forgiven yet. "After you saying you didn't love me last night and then spending the whole night carousing around town?"

Carousing? He was having a tough time looking away from her lips, which matched her dress. She'd dressed to kill today, and she was killing him. "I was in a holding cell all night."

Her eyes swept the deputies, and they both had the sense to look away. "I see."

Her blue gaze was direct and clear when it came back to him. "There's a ring in the jeweler's window, white gold, lots of tiny diamonds encrusted in a circular setting. Come home with that and maybe we'll talk." She pushed him off her and sashayed to the stairwell, every eye on her as she walked away. They'd already escorted Henriksson away in cuffs.

Cal sat up, feeling bruised and battered, but something inside him was bursting open—hope and sunshine even though it was a bitterly cold day. He yelled after her. "You're a little hard to impress, you know that, Dr. Sullivan?"

"Well, if you don't give it a try, I will," said one of the deputies with a grin.

Cal laughed. Because Sarah didn't want the deputy. She wanted *him*. He was finally getting it, after a lifetime of being denser than the resident mule on the ranch, something was finally getting through his thick skull. He. Deserved. To. Be. Happy. And so did she.

Nat held out his hand and hauled Cal to his feet. "She's stubborn."

Cal scratched his head. "I need to go get that ring."

"Damn right," said Nat.

Sheriff Talbot appeared on the roof and hitched his belt. "I need you two to come down to the station—"

Cal shook his head. "I need to get to the jewelers before it closes—"

"Too bad. You were involved in the apprehension of a gunman. What in the hell were you two doing up on the roof anyway?" Talbot eyed him, as if only just remembering he'd left him on the side of the road not twenty minutes ago.

For the first time ever, Cal got in Talbot's face. The fire inside him burned through the reserve he usually wore around the lawman. "Look, *Sheriff*, the woman I love could have died up here today, no thanks to you. She told me I need to go buy her diamonds, so I'm goddamned going to buy her diamonds."

Talbot squinted and ran his tongue over his teeth. "I'll take it under consideration, but for now, you're coming with me."

Nat stood beside him, tension radiating off him in waves. *Dammit*, Cal was done with all the bullshit he had to put up with. "No."

Talbot opened his mouth to argue or threaten.

Cal spoke over him. "I *get* that you need to question me." He wasn't an idiot. "I *get* that you think I'm scum of the earth for doing what any man would do when they saw another man whaling on a woman. There is nothing I can do to bring Terry's dad back from the dead, and believe me, I would if I could, just so he could get what he deserved instead of being treated like some innocent victim." The guy had been a vicious bully who used his fists on anything that caught his eye. Cal peered down at Talbot, no longer meek and mild, but gloriously pissed. "I can't change what you think about me, and I don't give a damn. But we're taking that trip to Stone Creek, and I'm doing a little shopping, right now, even if I have to go there in handcuffs. Otherwise, I'm gonna start pressing those charges of police harassment my lawyer suggested. Do you understand me?"

Talbot frowned and looked away. Then he nodded to one of the deputies. "Take Landon to the station in Stone Creek. Stop at Rozens' on the way. I'll question Mr. Sullivan first."

CHAPTER SEVEN

S ARAH'S BRAVADO EVAPORATED by the time she made it down to the admission desk. She found Madge stacking charts. "Anyone hurt?"

Madge shook her head. They both watched Henry Henriksson being placed into a police cruiser. Madge shifted her attention, sighed and fanned herself. "The only good thing about today is seeing all these fine men in uniform."

Sarah's knees started to collapse so she sank into the nurse's chair and bent over and hugged her legs. "I can't believe you're lusting after guys when we have bullet holes in the walls."

Madge chuckled and then gave another whistle. "Although Wrangler jeans work just fine too on a handsome cowboy. Hm, mmm."

"Tell me you aren't drooling over my brother."

"Him and his friend. Is he taken, sugar?"

Sarah scrambled to her feet in time to see Cal being forced into the back of another police cruiser. "He just saved my life on the roof." And told her he loved her. Her throat closed. "He's definitely taken." She wished the cops would stop harassing him.

Madge smiled slyly. "She's a lucky girl."

"I am." She caught Madge's dark eyes and grinned, even as tears started streaming down her face. "I really am." She cleared her throat and picked up a chart. "Okay then. I want to get home before Santa arrives with my presents, so let's get this chaos sorted and people out that door."

"You got it, doc." Madge gave her a wicked grin. "And, Sarah? Have fun opening your presents, honey."

"I intend to." Every day. She wasn't going to mess this up, even if Cal didn't bring her a ring, as long as he came home to her, she'd love him for the rest of their lives.

CAL WALKED OUT of his cabin, clean-shaven, wearing black dress pants and uncomfortable shoes that he'd bought for Nat and Eliza's wedding, a freshly ironed, blindingly white shirt, and a black Stetson. He took a deep breath. This was it.

"Sounds like you are preparing yourself for battle." A voice came out of the darkness.

He looked left and saw Sarah standing in the moonlight. She was wearing those boots again, and another red dress, but this one looked like it was made of wool and had long sleeves. His mouth went completely dry. His thoughts fried. He was pretty sure she was trying to kill him with longing and old-fashioned lust.

"Did I thank you for saving my life today?" she asked quietly.

"You're here, aren't you? That's all the thanks I

need." Knowing she was safe after that fuckwit had held a gun on her—sweet Jesus, he didn't want to think of it.

She moved closer, and he watched her carefully. She stood toe-to-toe with him and placed her hands on his chest, reached up on tiptoe and caught his lips with hers. She tasted like honey and cinnamon, smelled like apple pie.

He closed his eyes and kissed her back. God, he wanted her. Totally wanted her. Forever.

She pulled away. "I found this." She took the letter he'd left from her pocket. "You were leaving me."

He nodded.

"For my own good?"

He grimaced. "It seemed logical at the time."

Her eyes looked down at the frozen ground. No more snow yet, but Cal could smell it in the air.

"Does it seem logical now?" There were tears in her voice, and he hated that he'd hurt her, that he'd made her cry.

"No." He shook his head and caught her hand. Dropped to one knee. "Sarah Sullivan. Would you do me the very great honor of becoming my wife?" He pulled the small black velvet box from his back pocket and flipped it open. "I love you—which I also told you in the letter—and when I realized you were in danger today, I finally figured out I'm not responsible for everything that happens in this world, and I'd like to do my best to make you happy for as long as we've got."

Her hand trembled as she reached for the ring. "You found the one I wanted." She touched it reverently. "Oh, Cal, you didn't really have to get me a ring. I know how expensive it must have been."

Expensive? Did she really think he gave a damn about the money if this was the one she wanted? He took the ring out of the box and held it out.

She slipped it on her finger. "It fits."

"Is that a yes?"

She pressed her lips together while he held his breath. "Yes."

He whooped and jumped to his feet, sweeping her off hers and swinging her high into the air. "She said yes!" he shouted, and the echo bounced back at him from the hills.

He laughed when a cheer went up from down at the ranch house. He kissed her properly then and she kissed him back like she needed to climb inside him. He finally pulled back and looked at the ring sparkling on her finger. "I love you, Sarah Sullivan. As much as I'd like to go back to the cabin and peel off that dress inch by inch, I think we better go join the family."

She smiled up at him and touched his face. "How could you ever imagine I'd be better off without you?"

He touched his forehead to hers. "Cowboys aren't as smart as ER docs."

"Oh." Her eyes went wide. "I have something to tell you…" She took his hand and told him of her plans to take over the local family practice as they walked down the hill.

When they reached the main house the others rushed out of the front door and surrounded him with hugs and backslaps. How could he have believed he'd be able to leave this all behind? How could he have thought he had a right to make other people's decisions for them? They were all in this together. He glanced from Eliza's grinning face to Ryan's knowing smile. They'd been to hell and back and were still here fighting. Cal made his way to his fiancée, who was being hugged by her big brother. Cal tugged her away, picked her up, and kissed her thoroughly in front of everyone.

"Merry Christmas, Sarah," he said when they came up for air.

"Is Santa here yet, Unca Nat?" Tabitha piped up excitedly. None of the kids from the daycare had been hurt or had even heard gunfire, thank goodness.

Nat picked up his niece, tossed her in the air so she squealed with joy. "Not yet, kiddo. But Sarah and Cal both got to open one of their presents early. How about we all go peek under the tree and each sneak one present before we eat supper?"

Tabitha squealed and led the way. They all followed her into the den.

Sarah held Cal back for a moment and squeezed his hand. "I did get *exactly* what I wanted for Christmas." A light sparkled in her eyes just before she gave him another tender kiss on the side of his mouth. "And I'm not talking about the ring, cowboy."

Thank you for reading the *Her – Romantic Suspense* series. I hope you enjoyed it. I plan to include some of the other secondary characters in future books (Hello, FBI). Which reminds me, have you started the *Cold Justice* series yet? If not, continue reading the first chapter of my multi award-winning, bestselling Romantic Suspense novel,

A COLD DARK PLACE

LINDSEY KEEBLE SANG along to the radio, trying to pretend she wasn't freaked out by the dark. It was one in the morning and she hated driving this lonely stretch of highway between Greenville and Boden. Rain was threatening to turn to snow. The wind was gusting so forcefully that the tall trees looming high above her on the ridge made her swerve nervously toward the center line. The back tires slid on the asphalt and she slowed; no way did she want to wreck her precious little car.

She worked evenings at a gas station in Boden. It was quiet enough she usually got some studying done between customers. Tonight everyone and their dog were filling up ahead of a possible early winter storm. You'd think they'd never seen snow before.

A flash of red lights in her rearview had her heart squeezing. *Dammit!*

She hadn't been speeding—she couldn't afford a ticket and never drank alcohol. She signaled to pull over and stopped on the verge. Lindsey lived responsibly because she wanted a life bigger than her parochial hometown. She wasn't some hillbilly. She wanted to travel and see the world—Paris, Greece, maybe the pyramids if the unrest settled down. She peered through the sleet-drenched glass as a black SUV pulled in tight behind her.

A tall dark figure approached her vehicle. A cop's gold shield tapped against the glass. Frigid damp air flooded the interior as she rolled down the window and she huddled into her jacket as rain spat at her.

"License and registration." A low voice rumbled in that authoritative way cops had. He wore a dark slicker over black clothes. The gun on his hip glinted in the headlights of his vehicle. She didn't recognize his face, but then she couldn't really see his features with ice stinging her eyes.

"What's this about?" Her teeth chattered. She found the documents in her glove box and purse, and handed them over. Her hands returned to grip the hard plastic of the steering wheel as she waited. "I wasn't speeding."

"There's an alert out on a stolen red Neon so thought I'd check it out."

"Well, this is *my* car and I've done nothing wrong." She knew her rights. "You've got no reason to stop me."

"You were driving erratically." The voice got deeper and angrier. She winced. *Never piss off a cop*. "Plus, you've got a broken taillight. That gives me a reason."

Lindsey's worry was replaced by annoyance. She

snapped off her seat belt and applied the parking brake. She'd been shafted last year when another driver had sideswiped her in a parking lot and then claimed she'd been at fault to the insurers. "It was fine when I left for work this afternoon. I haven't hit anything in the meantime." *Goddamn it.*

"Go take a look." The cop stood back. He had a nice face despite the hard mouth and even harder eyes. Maybe she could sweet talk him out of a ticket, not that she was real good at sweet talk. Her dad could fix the light in the morning but if she had to pay a ticket as well, every hour of work today would have been for nothing.

She pulled the hood of her slicker over her head and climbed out. The headlights of his SUV blinded her as she took a few steps. She shielded her gaze and frowned. "I don't see anything—"

A surge of fire shot through her back. Pain exploded in a shockwave of screeching agony that overwhelmed her from the tips of her ears to the gaps between her toes. She'd never experienced anything like it. Sweat bloomed on her skin, clashing with sleet as she hit the tarmac. Rough hands grabbed her around the middle and hoisted her into the air. She couldn't control her arms or legs. She was shifted onto a hip where something unyielding bit into her stomach. She fought the urge to vomit even as her brain whirled.

It took a moment to make sense of what was happening.

This man wasn't a cop.

Still reeling from the stun gun, she couldn't get enough purchase to kick him, but she flailed at his knees and tried to elbow him in the balls. It didn't make any difference and she found herself dumped into the cold confines of the rear of his SUV. He zapped her again until her fillings felt like they were going to fall out and her bladder released.

The world tilted and she was on her front, face pressed into a dirty rubber mat, arms yanked behind her as something metal bit into one wrist, then the other. Handcuffs. *Oh, God.* She was handcuffed. A sharp pain ripped through her chest—if she didn't calm down she was going to die of a heart attack.

A ripping sound rang out in the darkness. She was shoved onto her back, and a piece of duct tape slapped over her mouth. It tangled with her hair and was gonna hurt like a bitch when it came off.

Something told her that was the least of her worries.

There was no reason for him to kidnap her unless he was going to hurt her. *Or kill her.*

The realization made everything stop. Every movement. Every frantic breath. Her heart raced and bile burned her throat as she stared into those cold, pitiless eyes. With a grunt he slammed the door closed, plunging her into a vast and consuming darkness. Rain beat the metal around her like an ominous drum. She was scared of the dark. Scared of monsters. Humiliated by the cold dampness between her legs. How could this have happened to her? One minute she was driving home, the next…

Where was her phone?

She rolled around, trying to feel it in her pockets. Shit. It was still in her purse in the passenger seat of her car. There was a crashing sound in the trees. She closed her eyes against the escalating panic. He'd gotten rid of her car. An elephant-sized lump threatened to choke her. She'd worked her ass off for that car, but finances and credit ratings were moot if she didn't survive this ordeal. This man was going to hurt her. She wriggled backward so her fingers could scrabble with the lock but there was nothing, and the panel above her head didn't budge even when she kicked it. *How dare he do this to me*? How dare he treat her as if she was nothing? She wanted to fight and rail against the injustice but as the SUV started up, she was immobilized by terror. All her life she'd fought to make things better, fought for a future and this man, this *bastard*, wanted to rip it all away from her. It wasn't fair. There had to be a way out. There had to be a way to survive.

She didn't want to die. She especially didn't want to die in the dark with a stranger who had eyes as cold as death. Tears brimmed. It wasn't fair. This wasn't fair.

A COLD DARK PLACE available now

Winner of the New England Readers' Choice Award and the Aspen Gold.
(**FREE** at the time of publication, but price subject to change without notice).

To find out what's next, sign up for Toni Anderson's newsletter to receive new release alerts, bonus scenes, and a free copy of The Killing Game:

www.toniandersonauthor.com/newsletter-signup

COLD JUSTICE WORLD OVERVIEW
All books can be read as standalones

COLD JUSTICE® SERIES
A Cold Dark Place (Book #1)
Cold Pursuit (Book #2)
Cold Light of Day (Book #3)
Cold Fear (Book #4)
Cold in The Shadows (Book #5)
Cold Hearted (Book #6)
Cold Secrets (Book #7)
Cold Malice (Book #8)
A Cold Dark Promise (Book #9~A Wedding Novella)
Cold Blooded (Book #10)

COLD JUSTICE® – THE NEGOTIATORS
Cold & Deadly (Book #1)
Colder Than Sin (Book #2)
Cold Wicked Lies (Book #3)
Cold Cruel Kiss (Book #4)
Cold as Ice (Book #5)

COLD JUSTICE® – MOST WANTED
Cold Silence (Book #1)
Cold Deceit (Book #2)
Cold Snap (Book #3) – Coming soon
Cold Fury (Book #4) – Coming soon

The Cold Justice® series books are also available as
audiobooks narrated by Eric Dove, and in various box
set compilations.

Check out all Toni's books on her website
(www.toniandersonauthor.com/books-2)

OTHER BOOKS BY TONI ANDERSON

ACKNOWLEDGMENTS

I wrote *Her Risk To Take* in response to readers asking me for more stories about the Triple H Ranch. When I originally wrote *Her Sanctuary* (it was my first book, took five years to write, and was originally published back in 2004) there was a third romance included within the book. I cut that subplot because the story was already complicated enough with Eliza and Nat's relationship, *and* Marsh and Josie's fumbled beginnings. What I hadn't realized until I reread *Her Sanctuary* was I'd taken out all hint of the feelings between Cal and Sarah. They'd lost their romance. Although I didn't feel as though I could create an entire novel around what happened next for those two characters, I did think they deserved their own "Happily Ever After." So the idea for this novella was born.

I want to thank my editor, Alicia Dean, and my amazing critique partner, Kathy Altman, for all their help and support on the original books. And thanks to Elaini Caruso who proofread the updated 2021 versions. The biggest shout-out of love and appreciation goes to my husband and children who put up with me on a daily basis, even when I don't have time to shower. Love you guys!

ABOUT THE AUTHOR

Toni Anderson writes gritty, sexy, FBI Romantic Thrillers, and is a *New York Times* and a *USA Today* bestselling author. Her books have won the Daphne du Maurier Award for Excellence in Mystery and Suspense, Readers' Choice, Aspen Gold, Book Buyers' Best, Golden Quill, National Excellence in Story Telling Contest, and National Excellence in Romance Fiction awards. She's been a finalist in both the Vivian Contest and the RITA Award from the Romance Writers of America. Toni's books have been translated into five different languages and over three million copies of her books have been downloaded.

Best known for her Cold Justice® books perhaps it's not surprising to discover Toni lives in one of the most extreme climates on earth—Manitoba, Canada. Formerly a Marine Biologist, Toni still misses the ocean, but is lucky enough to travel for research purposes. In late 2015, she visited FBI Headquarters in Washington DC, including a tour of the Strategic Information and Operations Center. She hopes not to get arrested for her Google searches.

Sign up for Toni Anderson's newsletter:
www.toniandersonauthor.com/newsletter-signup

Like Toni Anderson on Facebook:
facebook.com/toniandersonauthor

Follow on Instagram:
instagram.com/toni_anderson_author

Made in the USA
Middletown, DE
13 June 2024